WHISKING LOVE AND BUILDING DREAMS

THE SHOPS AT SUNSHINE BAY

JEANINE LAUREN

Littleford House Books

Whisking Love and Building Dreams

Copyright © 2025 by Jeanine Lauren

All rights reserved.

Whisking Love and Building Dreams was first published in Canada and around the world by Jeanine Lauren. This is a work of fiction. Similarities to real people, places, or events are entirely coincidental.

No part of this publication may be reproduced, stored in or introduced into a retrieval system, or transmitted in any form, or by any means (photocopying, electronic, recording, mechanical or otherwise) without the prior written approval of the copyright owner, except for the use of brief quotations in a book review.

ISBN: 978-1-997523-09-3

Cover Design by 100 Covers

CHAPTER 1

Esther Shepherd gripped the edge of the glossy reclaimed-wood counter of the Whisking Love Bakery and Bistro and surveyed the long line of customers that stretched out the front door. Any other spring day she'd be thrilled with the extra traffic, but today she was more concerned about getting through until closing time. With two servers down with the nasty flu sweeping Sunshine Bay, and the third, Nova, barely a week into the job, Esther was out front serving customers instead of in the back where she was most comfortable—cooking and baking and coming up with new variations she could serve throughout the week.

The familiar scents of the bistro—caramelized sugar, roasting coffee beans, and the yeasty comfort of rising dough—usually centered her, but today they mingled with the cloying perfume of too many customers in too small a space. The hiss of the espresso machine competed with the constant murmur of voices and the clatter of ceramic mugs against saucers. She absently wiped her brow with the back of her hand, realizing she had no idea what tomorrow's special would be. Normally by Tuesday afternoon, she'd have tested three new recipes, letting the seasonal ingredients inspire her. Instead, she was mechanically taking orders, her fingertips sticky with spilled syrup, her throat raw from calling out completed tickets, and her lower back screaming from standing all day at the espresso machine.

When the rush was over in the afternoon, she would have to train Nova to turn out lattes and other drinks with the signature hearts—and, this month, cats—in the froth on top. Normally she would leave the training to Jessica or Blake, but Jessica had been away for two days already and now Blake was out too. Both sounded horrible, and she couldn't have them back at work, much less anywhere near customers, until they were healthy again. She would have to find someone to help for the next few days because Nova was looking like an overwhelmed deer in the headlights and Esther was feeling the burn on the bottom of her feet from standing too long.

She looked up at the line again and her heart jumped in her chest. Standing there was her big brother Rick, who always seemed to bring drama with him in the form of his wife Dana. Esther really didn't have time for Dana right now. Her hands trembled slightly as she scanned the room for her sister-in-law but, finding no sign of her, she met Rick's gaze, fighting the collision of emotions: the joy of seeing her brother after years of virtual silence, and the resentment she still felt at his abandonment. What could have brought him here without even a phone call to warn her?

"Hi, Esther," he said, leaning with one hand on the counter, a backpack slung over his shoulder. His other hand dragged a large rolling suitcase.

He'd grown older since she'd last seen him four years earlier. Older than his fifty-two years. But he was still fit, thanks to years of physical labor, and when he smiled, the dimples they had both inherited from their mother showed in his cheeks.

"Rick," she said calmly, training her eyes on him directly instead of the accompanying luggage. Surely they didn't intend to stay with her tonight. She wasn't in the mood, especially after so many years of him communicating only in Christmas cards and the occasional text on her birthday.

"Sorry I didn't call," he said, speaking low enough that those in line couldn't hear them. "But you'll be happy to know that I finally understand what you were on about. I've left Dana."

Well, that changed things. She gave him a quick smile. "You need a place to stay."

"Just until I get on my feet again. I didn't know where else to go."

She looked at him more closely, ignoring the shifting feet of the waiting customers behind him. His curly black hair was now streaked with silver, and he hadn't shaved in days. Maybe he was growing his beard in again. The thought made her smile. Dana had hated his beard.

"Have you eaten?" she asked.

"Not since breakfast on the plane."

"Sit down at the staff table." She nodded toward a table tucked up near the end of the counter, out of the way of the customers. "I'll get you a soup and sandwich. It's mushroom today—you still like mushroom?"

"Thanks, sis," he said nodding gratefully.

"It'll be a while." She gestured at the line behind him. "We're busy, and I'm short-staffed today."

"That's okay."

"Here." She drew a mug out from near the counter and poured him a coffee from the pot. "Take this. The cream and sugar are at the other end of the counter. And hang on a minute." She put a blueberry scone, an old favorite of his, onto a plate and slid it toward him. "You can stow your gear in the hall under the coatrack. It'll be out of the way there."

"I'll be back in a minute." He pulled his belongings into the hallway and returned to pick up the coffee and scone.

She smiled at him and patted his hand. "It's good to see you. I'll join you as soon as I can."

Then she returned to the line of people, and together with Nova they rang up orders. Nova picked up from the kitchen while Esther made the coffee drinks and considered where to get more temporary help.

She considered calling Soo Yin, who normally came in on Wednesdays, the one day she had off from her courses at the university. But she was taking final exams this month and likely wouldn't have time. If it were June, Esther could get her mother to come in, but her parents were in Costa Rica for another month. Maybe she could call one of her friends to help? She kept pondering until, twenty minutes later, there was a break in the steady stream of drink orders, and she could see how Nova was hanging in.

"You're doing well," she told the young woman, who had only started a week prior.

Nova smiled. "Thanks, but I haven't had time to wipe tables yet."

"How about I give you a hand with that?" said a deep voice from the other side of the counter.

She turned to look at Rick, who had inhaled the soup and sandwich she had passed to him between orders.

"You sure?"

He looked at her, one eyebrow raised in a way that said, *seriously?* "You don't think I can still do it? Clearing tables can't be that different from thirty years ago."

"It would be a big help if you cleared the tables and took the dishes to the back. At least the dishwasher and the kitchen staff came in today."

"I'm on it," he said, walking toward the bin of dishes at the end of the counter. He came back a few minutes later with an empty bin, a cloth, and a spray bottle of sanitizer, and made quick work of busing and wiping down any of the tables that were left dirty by customers.

Esther watched him for a moment, remembering the years they had worked together in the bistro after school, on weekends, and over all the holidays. Their parents had believed a family business meant the whole family worked in the business as a team. And it had been that way until she left to marry Seth and Rick moved to Edmonton to work in the oil fields as an electrician. He'd then moved on to commercial buildings, earned his ticket as a journeyman, and set up his own shop closer to home, working on a mix of builds.

He moved around the room as though he hadn't been gone all that time, and she smiled. Maybe with Dana gone, there was a chance for them to reconnect. She had missed him.

The stream of customers had slowed to a trickle, so she told Nova to order her lunch and take a break while she cleaned up the counter and added more baked goods to the display area.

A group of tourists was already congregating outside, loudly asking how to get to the beach. It was a sure sign that the season was accelerating.

The afternoon coffee crowd would soon descend upon the cinnamon sticky buns and lavender-infused teacakes that had earned Whisking Love a mention in *Pacific Living* magazine the summer before. She made a mental note to order extra ingredients in anticipation of the tour buses that visited from Victoria and transformed their peaceful village into a bustling summer getaway. There were two seasons in Sunshine Bay—winter, and tourist—and tourist season was ramping up weeks ahead of schedule.

"Who's your new helper?" asked a familiar voice. She looked up to see her friend Curtis, in jeans and a well-worn blue checked shirt, leaning on the counter.

"My brother Rick. He just arrived."

"That's Rick? You didn't tell me he was coming," said Curtis, smiling at her in that way that always made her feel seen. "Maybe I'll finally get to meet him."

"I didn't know he was coming. He showed up around an hour ago. I haven't seen him in four years," she confided.

"Wow, that's a long time." Curtis's brow wrinkled in thought.

"Well, he's been living back east with his wife, and with the business, I haven't been able to travel for years." She didn't mention that visiting Dana was the last thing she would ever want to do on her time off.

"How long is he here?"

"I have no idea," said Esther. "We've been pretty busy the last few hours, so I haven't been able to ask."

"At least he knows his way around the bistro."

"That he does. Mom and Dad made sure we both knew the restaurant business. Can I get you anything?"

"Coffee. And what's your soup and sandwich?"

"Cream of mushroom and a toasted Reuben. Or you can have a grilled veggie if you prefer."

"I'll take the Reuben and the soup, and a coffee, of course."

"Of course," said Esther. Curtis had what could only be called an addiction to the black brew.

"I was also going to ask you if you'd like to come with me to see a movie tonight, but I didn't know you had company."

"Don't let me cramp your style," said Rick, who had just approached the counter after setting an empty bin near the door where people could put their dishes. "I took the long way here. Six-hour layover in Calgary and another two in Vancouver, not to mention the pleasure of sitting next to a woman with a colicky newborn. I'm planning to sleep as soon as business slows down and Esther doesn't need any more help."

Right. She had to think about where to bed him down for the night. Her apartment was in a bit of a tangle, but she could shift some of the boxes she had been storing in her spare room so he could at least use the fold-out couch. Not great, but then he hadn't warned her he was coming, had he?

"Rick, this is my friend Curtis Woodrow. We often go to the movies on Tuesday nights because I close at five that day and they have an early show."

"Two-for-one popcorn on Tuesdays is also nothing to sneeze at," Curtis said, his brown eyes crinkling in a face more weathered by sun than by age. "Your sister is a popcorn fiend."

"Only when it has a lot of butter," added Esther.

Rick laughed. "You haven't changed on that score. What's playing?"

"A thriller—I can't remember the name," said Curtis, turning his gaze toward Esther. "It's that one we saw the trailer for a couple of weeks ago."

"Oh, right. That did look good. But I'm not sure I can go tonight. I've had fewer staff than normal, and I have to be up early tomorrow to do some extra baking."

"I can give you a hand in the morning," said Rick. "It'll give us a chance to catch up. I'll be out for the count once I hit the pillow tonight."

She looked at Rick and then at Curtis and sighed. "Okay. Why don't you pick me up at six-thirty and we'll walk over together?"

Curtis beamed. "I'll be here." He took the coffee that Esther had poured for him, and she watched his wiry frame glide to his regular table, stopping to chat with some of the customers along the way.

"Esther's got a boyfriend," Rick whispered, in the same teasing lilt he'd used when they were teenagers.

She scowled. "You haven't changed." She busied herself wiping down the spotless counter. "Curtis is… complicated."

"Complicated, huh?" Rick chuckled. "That's what people say when they're avoiding the truth."

"He's just an old high school friend who lost his wife a few years ago. I've been helping him get through his grief. We've known each other a long time."

"Uh-huh," said Rick in a tone that said, *Sure, sis, keep telling yourself that.*

"Really, there's nothing between us except friendship. He was, and is, in love with his wife. They were high-school sweethearts, and I knew her through choir.

That's all there is to it." Though sometimes when he looked at her with that warm smile of his, she hoped there could be more. But then she'd remember he smiled at everyone. That was just the kind of person he was. And he wasn't interested in anything more.

"Well, from the look on his face, I beg to differ."

Esther turned to see what Rick was looking at and saw Curtis gazing in her direction as he often did when he sat at his regular table.

"He looks like he's hungry," said Rick.

"He is. That's why he ordered lunch. And now he's considering what he wants for dessert." She pointed at the pastry display in front of her.

"Yes, I believe you're right about that," said her brother. He chuckled and waggled his eyebrows at her, and she had the sudden urge to smack him on the arm like she used to do when he teased her.

"Don't make me regret my decision to let you stay with me," she said in a low voice.

He just laughed louder. "It's good to be back, Esther. I've missed you." And he pulled her in for a big bear hug, a gesture that felt both welcome and foreign. She hugged him back, startled by the brother who'd once avoided physical affection. How long had it been since she'd really hugged someone? Maybe they could get back to their old relationship now that Dana was out of the picture. She really had missed him.

CHAPTER 2

Curtis watched Esther and her brother talking at the front counter. He'd never met Rick, who had left town after graduating high school two years before Curtis's family moved to town.

And Esther hadn't mentioned her brother in years. In fact, every time he brought up anything about him, she changed the subject. And yet here were Rick and Esther, sharing a hug, smiling, laughing. She did look a little guarded, however. He hoped that her brother's return would be a good thing.

But he didn't have a lot of time to think about Esther or her brother just then. His friend Jack Robertson, who was meeting him for lunch, had just walked through the door. Curtis stood, shook Jack's hand, and asked the older man if he wanted something to eat.

"I've got it," said Jack, waving him away and walking up to the counter to put in his order. He walked back a few moments later with a latte and a piece of cheese-cake covered in fruit.

"Looks good," said Curtis. "I should have ordered that too."

"Don't tell Sylvia. She's got me eating healthy food again."

Curtis shook his head. "I've eaten Sylvia's healthy food. You've got nothing to complain about, my friend."

Jack chuckled. "I know. I'm a lucky man to have stumbled upon that woman. She saved me."

"Yes, nothing like having a partner you can count on," said Curtis, remembering Maggie with gratitude. He waited to feel the familiar tightness in his chest, the constriction in his throat that had been his constant companion for years. But where sharp pain once lived there was only a gentle warmth. When had he stopped having trouble thinking about Maggie? And why hadn't he noticed? His fingers trembled slightly as he set down his cup, unsettled by the realization that he was healing in ways he hadn't recognized. He felt a rush of relief, and then a pang of guilt for moving forward, as though by doing so betrayed her memory. Hadn't he encouraged his friend Rob to do just that a few weeks earlier? Rob was dating, and even risking love again. But Rob was ready. Curtis wasn't.

"Sorry. Didn't mean to bring up the past," said Jack.

"You know me," said Curtis. "I'm not afraid of difficult topics. How else could I run the Shack?" Curtis was the coordinator of the local Men's Shack, where older men came together to work on community projects, their own projects, and to just shoot the breeze with others. It was Sunshine Bay's answer to reducing loneliness in men—a problem that, to Curtis's mind, had become an epidemic in North America.

"True," said Jack. "Though listening to someone's troubles is different than sharing your own."

Curtis didn't say anything, just thanked his lucky stars that he still had Jack to support him with the Shack. He was a real gem.

Nova, the young woman at the counter who sported spiky green hair and a nose ring, called out his order. Curtis crossed to the counter, breathing in the rich aroma of freshly ground coffee beans and the buttery scent of pastries still warm from the oven. The gentle hum of conversation mingled with the rhythmic hiss of the espresso machine and the soft clinking of ceramic mugs. He picked up his sandwich and crossed the honey-brown floorboards back to his seat. Where he kept looking at Esther while Jack told him about the new project the local naturalist society had approached him with. Today Esther was wearing a white T-shirt and black pants, her mass of sandy-brown curls swept up in an effortless bun. He liked her hair like that but preferred it when it fell below her shoulders. What would it be like to touch, he wondered, but he shook that notion away. Esther was his friend, and he needed her.

What would he have done without her and her way of putting people at ease? When she reentered his life several years earlier as part of Maggie's choir, she had supported Maggie through her illness. Later, she had supported him. Long after others had scattered back to their own lives, it was only Esther, and some men from the local grief support group, who had stuck by him through his long struggle.

How many times had he talked to Esther about his boys? Anthony and Logan had struggled with their mother's death and with stepping out into the world—Logan headed off to Vancouver for university as soon as he turned eighteen, hoping to become a doctor like his mother, and Anthony had returned a year after gaining his diploma in sound engineering to live at home with Curtis. He often wondered if Ant would still be living at home if Maggie had lived.

He would never know.

"I found a pattern for the bat houses," said Jack, pulling Curtis back to the conversation.

"Bat houses?"

"Yes." Jack wrinkled his brow at Curtis. "Weren't you listening?"

"Sorry, I was momentarily distracted," said Curtis, rubbing his head of short graying hair and turning his full attention toward Jack. It didn't pay to have the man think he didn't care to listen. Especially when he seemed so excited about these bat house things.

Jack narrowed his eyes at Curtis, as though ensuring he was indeed now listening, before he launched into his story of a woman who'd asked if he could help make bat boxes for a bat garden they were building in the community garden.

"Bat garden?" Curtis asked.

"Basically, it's an organic garden, with some water for the critters, without cats roaming around, and with bat houses—places for them to roost and raise their young."

"How many bat houses do they want?"

"They figure about a dozen. It's for the community garden down by the tracks. And they'll want pup catchers added, of course."

"Pup catchers?"

"It's a screen you can put at the bottom of the house to catch any pups that fall. They're hoping to have a few babies."

"When do they need these boxes and… what did you call them? Pup catchers?"

"I figure we could get them done in about two weeks.

Spoke to Stan and his two friends who recently joined. They're keen to help."

"Any special materials?"

"Nothing that can't be sourced at the local shop. They expect to have the money raised for that by the end of May. They're counting on a grant. We just need to provide the labor and tools."

"It sounds like a good idea," said Curtis. "Any time we can help the environment, and the city, is an opportunity to keep our organization in public view."

"And an opportunity to recruit new members and volunteers," said Jack, grinning. "Don't think I hadn't thought of that."

"I hope you're right," said Curtis, smiling at Jack's contagious optimism. The man had spent most of his work life in banking, whereas Curtis was more than familiar with the struggle of having to piece together enough funding to keep his organizations going. This one, and the ones he had worked with prior to Maggie's death.

"Here." Jack rooted in the pocket of his coat and pulled out a piece of paper, which he spread out on the table in front of them.

"What's this?"

"A bat box pattern," said a man's voice. Jack and Curtis looked up to see Esther's brother Rick standing there.

"You know about them?" asked Jack.

"I made a few when I was living in Nova Scotia as part of a service club project."

"Well, if you want to help us, come on down to the Shack," said Jack, pulling a card out of his pocket and handing it to Rick.

Rick took it and looked at the card. "A Men's Shack, eh?" Rick was looking at Curtis, and Curtis had the distinct feeling that he was being weighed and measured.

"It's a good place to meet people. And I'm Jack, by the way." He put out his hand.

"Rick." They shook. "I'm just in town for a bit, visiting my sister."

"Well, if you're still around in a few weeks we could use a hand with the boxes. None of us have made them before."

"Where did you get the pattern?" asked Rick, his posture relaxing slightly at the familiar topic. "I know there's one with a lot of research behind it, from one of the national conservation agencies."

"Yes," said Jack. "That's what I discovered too. This is the one they recommended."

Rick nodded approvingly, then glanced over his shoulder at Esther, who was studiously avoiding looking their way. His expression softened with something that looked like regret. "Well, if I'm still in town, I'd love to help. Right now…" He hesitated, choosing his words carefully. "I'm focusing on what Esther needs. She's down a few staff this week, and she looks exhausted."

"Sure," said Jack, friendly as aways. Curtis had rarely ever seen him upset.

"Meanwhile, I'll pick up your dishes if you've finished with them," said Rick. He reached for the plates and bowl. "And thanks for the card and the offer," he added. "If I'm still here, I'll think about it."

They watched him walk away, and Jack said, "I didn't even know Esther had a brother."

"He hasn't been around much," said Curtis. "Lives on the other end of the country, I think."

"Well, it's nice he's here to help her. Since her parents retired and left this place with her, I sometimes wonder how she keeps going. Especially since so many of her staff are in college and work only part-time."

"She's pretty driven," said Curtis, looking at Esther. His sister was showing Nova how to make a decoration on the coffee drink she was crafting. As he watched, Rick approached them, saying something that made Esther's smile falter momentarily before she recovered. Curtis felt a protective instinct stir within him. He'd spent years learning to read Esther's subtle expressions, and whatever Rick had just said had clearly unsettled her.

He continued to watch Esther out of the corner of his eye. Nova was concentrating hard, carefully following Esther's instructions. Then she looked up at Esther with a grin, and Esther gave her a high five. *Nice*, he thought. *That's a lesson Nova won't forget soon.*

It was so typically Esther—finding teaching moments in everyday tasks, celebrating small victories. Unlike other bosses who'd micromanage or criticize, Esther built confidence with patience and genuine enthusiasm. The café wasn't just her business; it was her way of stitching the community together, one conversation and artisan coffee at a time.

"Driven or not, Esther takes on a lot of responsibility," said Jack, and Curtis shifted his gaze back to his table mate. "She's president of the downtown business association again this year, with all the side projects that entails. She's part of the choir. And she's running this place, training new staff, coming up with new menus, welcoming twice the number of tour buses as last year. It must get exhausting. Hopefully her brother will stay on a while. Give her a bit of help for a change."

Curtis looked steadily at his friend. "I never thought about how tired she must get." In fact, she'd said she was tired today, and yet he'd still pushed her to go out with him. A twinge of self-reproach tightened his shoulders. For years, he'd been the one needing support, and Esther had given it freely. Now that he was finally emerging from his grief, he'd immediately asked for more of her time without considering her needs. Should he cancel? He looked over at her, still busy with customers, and decided to give her the option to cancel that evening instead.

"It's Sylvia's influence," said Jack.

"What is?"

"Since she came into my life, she's taught me a thing or two about people. She notices others, and it's rubbing off, I think. If I'd noticed earlier, maybe my wife wouldn't have left me. But then I wouldn't have Sylvia, either." He laughed a self-deprecating laugh, but Curtis knew the truth. Jack had a knack for helping others when they didn't even know they needed help. He wished he had more neighbors like Jack.

"Well, here's to Sylvia," said Curtis, raising his coffee cup. "May she continue to rub off on you for many years to come."

"Hear, hear," said Jack, smiling and raising his cup as well. Then he turned back to his new favorite subject. "Did I show you how the pup catchers work yet? They're quite ingenious."

"Do tell," said Curtis, chuckling. As he listened to his friend explain the catchers, out of the corner of his eye he watched Esther set out a cup of coffee and a bowl of soup and join her brother at the staff table. She did look tired. Maybe there was something he could help her with.

He would have to ask tonight if he got the chance. After all the times she'd sat and listened to him go on and on about his grief—and his troubles with being a lone parent to his growing sons—she hadn't once said she didn't have time for him.

Well, now that he was stronger, maybe there was a way he could help her. He would find a way to return the favor.

CHAPTER 3

"It's good to see you," said Esther as she sat down with Rick, noticing the new creases at the corners of his eyes, the gray streaks in his dark curls. She slid his coffee toward him. "Thanks for all your help today."

Rick wrapped his calloused hands around the mug. "It was like old times," he said, a half-smile playing at the corner of his mouth. "Except without Dad standing over us, monitoring our movements."

Esther laughed, the sound catching slightly in her throat. "He drove us hard, didn't he? 'Time is money, Essie.'" She mimicked their father's gruff baritone, and the nickname he'd only used when particularly pleased with her work.

"He drove us out the door," said Rick with a frown. He traced a circle on the wooden tabletop. "And look what that got him. Thirty years of sixty-hour weeks and a heart that gave out before he hit sixty-five."

Esther saw a shadow of guilt cross Rick's face—the same shadow she fought whenever she stayed past midnight balancing the books. Some legacies were harder to escape than others.

"I know. I often wonder if he hadn't been so type A, would he have had that heart problem? But then, who knows what I would have ended up doing if he hadn't?"

"Maybe you would have found yourself a nice cushy office job," said Rick.

"With a sore bum from sitting instead of so much pressure on my feet," said Esther, laughing. Today her feet ached more than usual. She would have to replace the anti-fatigue mats in front of the coffee machine or get some new shoes. Or both.

"I hear you. Physical labor can take its toll on a body," said Rick. "There are some jobs I can't do anymore. Especially if they involve kneeling." He rubbed his knees to demonstrate his pain.

"What are your plans?" asked Esther. She hadn't counted on her brother just showing up. Then again, she couldn't just push him away either. She owed him so much.

"I walked away," he said. "Left her with everything but some of my retirement savings."

"After what she put you through?"

"It wasn't worth it, Esther. I just wanted out."

"What about the boys?"

"Sean has taken over the business. He still calls me for advice, so we at least have a relationship, strained as it is."

"And Cameron?"

"I don't know where he is. He hasn't been home in three years. Once he finished school, he got work out west somewhere."

"Is that why you're here? To track down Cameron?"

Rick brushed his hand through his hair. "I know he had a job working audio on some 'Hollywood North' set last year, but something Sean said to me last week has led me to think he's in trouble."

"What kind of trouble?"

"Not sure, but Sean said Cameron called him for money a few months ago. He couldn't pay his rent."

"Why didn't he call you?"

"According to Sean, he did. He asked Dana, and she told him never to contact us for money again." Rick looked at Esther, his eyes sadder than she had ever seen them. "Dana never even told me he'd called, and that was months ago. I haven't heard from him since just after Christmas. It was the last straw. I've called him repeatedly, but he isn't picking up. I confronted Dana, and she was horrible. Went on about how her kids were such ungrateful sods. I couldn't believe it. They're good guys, Esther."

Esther reached across the table and patted him on the arm. "I know they're good kids." Inside, she was thinking, *Finally. Maybe this will be the time it will stick.* "What does Sean think?"

"He seemed relieved that I was planning to leave Nova Scotia. Asked me if I wanted back into the business. He's enjoying being the boss."

"Well, you can stay with me as long as you need to,"

she said. "I'll close up in an hour and then get you settled into the apartment."

"Thanks. I'm just glad to be home," he said. "I know it sounds odd after I've been away for so long, but it still feels like home here."

Esther wanted to ask what had possessed him to leave Dana the house and their assets and just walk away, though she had a feeling she knew the answer. Sometimes you just had to make a clean break and start over.

"Where do you think Cameron is?" she asked.

"I think he's still in Vancouver. I've texted him. Told him what happened between his mother and me. Told him I was coming here for a while. Asked him to join me if he wanted to."

"Has he answered you?"

"No. But Sean talked to him. Assured him that we were splitting up. That his mother's opinion wasn't shared by me. The ball's in his court for now."

"That's all you can do right now, then," said Esther.

"What I need to do now is find some work and a place to live. I was looking at work out in the oil fields again, but that's a younger man's game. My body is just too wrecked for that. It was great when I was raising kids, and it earned me the money I needed to buy our house, but I hated it. I want something in a warmer climate now. Somewhere I can work with younger folks, maybe."

"Do you want to stay here? I mean find a job in town? Or do you want to move elsewhere?" She noticed the confusion on his face and immediately backtracked. "Sorry, too much too soon. You probably haven't even thought that far ahead."

"No, I haven't. One step at a time. I just got the guts to leave, Esther. It was harder than I thought it would be."

"Are you regretting the decision?"

"No," he said flatly. "Once I saw her through my sons' eyes, saw what she had done to them by being so self-absorbed, it was as though someone finally shone a light onto all the broken bits of our marriage, and I couldn't unsee them again."

"I can't believe you left her the house and every-thing," she said, going back on her own promise not to get into the details.

"Well, I didn't exactly leave her everything," he said, leaning forward and speaking quietly. "When Sean and I started the business a few years ago, we never put her name on it. Told her it was better for her tax-wise if we didn't. So I have half the business, and it's doing well. Sean is buying me out slowly, and I'm putting that money toward an investment."

"So you must have known on some level that you needed to protect yourself," she mused.

"Maybe," he said, sitting back. "I'd like to think that. But it was Sean who insisted that only the pair of us be involved. I just agreed because it seemed to mean so much to him, and Dana doesn't know anything about being an electrician."

"No, she's a beautician," said Esther. Which, given the permanent sneer on her sister-in-law's face, always fascinated her. How could someone so bent on making other people's lives miserable be in the beauty business?

"For now."

"Is her business in trouble?"

"No, quite the contrary. But I hear from Sean that she's selling it, and probably the house, and moving to a condo. Retiring, apparently. Living half the year in Florida."

"And leaving her youngest son to flounder?"

"No. Leaving it to me to fix. She thinks I wasn't as involved as I should have been when they were younger and now it's my turn. Maybe she's right."

"I don't know what you ever saw in Dana."

"She has her plusses." He picked up his coffee cup and drained it. "We had fun for our first few years. And she was driven enough to start a business and expand it to three locations. Taught me what I needed to do to get ahead. She's talented. Driven. She's just not very maternal and has different values than I do."

"It's not fair how those who like kids can't have them, and those who dislike them don't appreciate them," said Esther.

"She does love her children. She just doesn't believe in helping what she calls 'grown men'. That is where we differ, I suppose. But, no, life isn't fair, Esther. And I'm sorry you never had children. You'd have been a great mother."

"Thanks," said Esther quietly. "Some things are just not meant to be, I suppose." She looked past Rick's shoulder to where Nova was cleaning the espresso machine. "But at least I'm able to help a whole crew of teens and twenty-somethings with their first jobs," she said, forcing brightness into her voice. She had come to terms with not having children years earlier, but sometimes regret seeped back into her mind for a few moments.

She straightened her shoulders. "Speaking of which, I'm going to check in on Nova and the kitchen crew and make sure they've started on cleanup for the day. Want another cup of coffee?"

"Just a glass of water. If I take in any more caffeine, I'll be climbing the walls instead of getting to sleep."

"By the way, the room upstairs will need some shifting," she warned. "I have a bunch of supplies stored up there. Had a bit of a problem in the storeroom and had to move boxes there temporarily."

"I just need a bed," said Rick. "We can worry about next steps tomorrow."

"Do you think you'll stay on for a while?"

"I don't honestly know," he said. "I need to find work, and I need to connect with Cameron. Then I'll have a better idea of what to do."

"Well, meanwhile, it's good to have you here. I can use your help this week if you're around," said Esther, bending to give him a quick hug.

"Thanks, sis," he whispered, and she could tell he was close to tears.

"And I'll do everything I can to help you," she said.

"You don't have to worry about me. That's not why I came."

"Nonsense. We're family. And after what you did for me…" She let the words hang between them, heavy with the weight of the unspoken past. They never talked about it directly—not the hospital, not the way Rick had come when she called for help, not the way he'd kept her with him through those dark months after.

"You would have been just fine," he said, though she knew she owed him her life. Esther swallowed hard. She'd spent fifteen years rebuilding and distancing herself from the woman she'd been that night, but she still sometimes needed to remind herself that she was okay—or distract herself with work, which seemed like a good idea right now.

"The water is in that urn." She pointed to the other end of the counter as she rose to return to the kitchen. "I'll see you in a bit."

She walked over to see how Nova was doing, leaving Rick to ponder his next steps. But she was glad she could at least give him a soft place to land in the meantime. And a soft bed—once they found it beneath all those boxes.

CHAPTER 4

Curtis followed the weathered brick exterior of the building till he came to the back, where the door to the apartments above Whisking Love were located. The sun was low in the sky, and the light caught the metal panel of the apartment call box, turning it copper-gold. He liked this time of year, when the days grew longer and people seemed to be lighter and more relaxed after the long gray winter.

He climbed the stairs to the apartments above, each step creaking in familiar places. The hallway stretched before him—a gauntlet of sensations. Discordant notes from the beginner's piano class in Making Sweet Music drifted up through the floorboards. "Für Elise." A song he recognized from when his own sons had practiced it repeatedly on the piano, before they took up their guitars.

The rich scent of chocolate wafted from the new shop just beyond, undercut with the sharper tang of the raspberry filling they'd been experimenting with this week. Emma, the chocolatier, had offered him samples twice, and he'd been happy to accept. His son Anthony had been even happier that he'd brought home a box of them.

At the end of the hall, he stood in front of Esther's door. Four years of standing at this same threshold, always as a friend in need, never really seeing beyond his own grief. He straightened his shoulders and knocked, the sound unexpectedly loud in the quiet hallway.

Esther answered, dressed in a pair of jeans and a striped shirt, her long curls hanging loose around her shoulders as though she were granting him his wish from earlier. She looked relaxed and not as exhausted as she had appeared earlier.

"Hi there," she said. "Come on in for a minute. We're just moving some stuff to make room for Rick."

Curtis stepped into the little hallway that he knew led past bedrooms to the living room and kitchenette, though he had only been inside a handful of times, and never for longer than a few minutes.

And never when the place looked so disorganized.

"What's all this?" he asked, glancing around at piles of boxes.

"I ordered extra supplies last month in anticipation of the summer rush. I intended to put the in the store-room but… Never mind. I haven't got round to shifting it, that's all."

"But don't the deliveries come to the café?"

"Yes," she said, her face reddening. "I got these delivered up here."

"Why?"

"Because I haven't finished setting up the storeroom yet," she said.

"Yet?"

"What is this? The third degree?" Her face was shuttered, which made him curious.

"Did something happen, Esther?"

She sighed. "Last weekend. After your Making Music for a Cause fundraiser. I came back to find a small flood in the back room."

"A flood? Why didn't you tell me?"

She looked at him strangely, and it gave him pause. Why *would* she call him? *He* was the one who had relied on *her* all these years. *She* was the one who listened to his deepest concerns.

Why had he never noticed that she rarely shared anything about herself? Four years of conversations across her café tables, hundreds of hours of her listening to his pain, his struggles, his slow journey back to himself—and he couldn't recall a single instance where she'd truly opened up about her own troubles. Not even about things he was clearly in a position to assist with, like building repairs.

Memories surfaced in rapid succession: Esther at Maggie's funeral, a package of tissues at the ready, organizing the catering herself, leaving no detail undone so that he and his sons needn't concern themselves with anything; Esther bringing food to them—casseroles that could be reheated or artisan pizza from her shop; Esther remembering her sons' birthdays, his anniversary, and all the first and second anniversaries—the first being hardest, the second, a little easier; Esther helping him with their annual fundraiser for cancer research, Making Music for a Cause. She had been there for him all those times.

Always giving. Always helping others.

He had always considered them to be friends—close friends—but, standing in her cluttered hallway, he suddenly felt like a stranger. Esther had a lot of friends. She greeted dozens of people by name each day at the café, and kept track of their lives with uncanny precision. She probably called someone else when she needed help. Someone she trusted more than him.

The thought stung.

"I called my insurance agent," she said. "They sent out a restoration company, mopped it up, and fixed the leaky pipe. I threw out a few boxes of paper cups that were on the ground, but I haven't had a chance to organize the storeroom yet. Hence, this." She cast out her arm at the piles of boxes.

"Do you need help?" Curtis looked over her head at Rick, who shrugged his shoulders and shook his head.

"I'll get to it," she said. "We've just been busier than I expected the past few weeks."

"Okay," said Curtis, "but I can give you a hand if you like."

"What is it with you? Don't you know how to take no for an answer?" she snapped.

"Right. Sorry." He took a step back and waited. She was on edge, and he felt guilty about asking her to go to the movie now.

"No, I'm sorry. I shouldn't have snapped. It's just been a long week, and it's only Tuesday."

"I can take a rain check on the movie if you like."

"Actually, it might be good to get a start on clearing this out," said Esther, looking around the room as though she was afraid the boxes would attack her.

"Not a chance." Rick walked behind Esther and set a box atop another in the hallway. "I've found the sofa bed, cleared enough room to open it, and now, if you tell me where to get the bedding and a towel, I'm going to sleep. You and Curtis should go out and enjoy yourselves. Leave me to get my beauty sleep."

"There's not much you can do here tonight anyway," said Curtis, hopeful that she would be convinced to come with him. "Not if Rick is sleeping."

"I'll help you tomorrow," said Rick. "I'll take a look at the storage room and figure out what you need."

"Shelves, mostly," said Esther. "I should have more that are higher off the floor, just in case it happens again. The building is old. They said it was likely a one-off, but you never know about these things."

"Shelves are an easy fix, sis," said Rick.

"And if you need some help," said Curtis, looking at Rick and then glancing down to Esther, "let me know. I have some free time now that the fundraiser is over, and I'm looking for a project for one of my crews at the Shack."

Esther opened her mouth to protest and then looked between them and smiled. "Looks like I'm outnumbered on this. Yes, I will go to the movie and, yes, I will accept your help, both of you. I thought I could do it myself, but with the staff off sick and work to be done for the downtown business association, I'm swamped."

"Good, that's settled," said Rick. "Now I believe you need to leave, or you're going to be late for the show."

She grinned and gave her brother a spontaneous hug, one that left Curtis feeling like an outsider.

"It's good to have you back," she said to Rick. "I've missed you."

"Good to be back," said Rick, though Curtis noticed a shadow around Rick's eyes. The man was obviously tired, but Curtis didn't think it was just a physical exhaustion. He knew that look because he had seen it in the mirror often in the past four years. Grief. Loss. Hopelessness. Loneliness. The marks of a man who had lost his footing and wasn't sure where to turn next. Maybe this was something Curtis could do to help. If he got to know Rick, helped him find his way, that would help Esther.

And maybe she would let him into her life just a little more.

"I'll get you that bedding and feed Pearl," said Esther, walking further into the apartment.

"Pearl?" asked Rick.

"It's a white rescue cat she got a few years ago," said Curtis.

"How come I haven't seen it?"

"It's a skittish thing," said Curtis. "Probably hiding right now. I've only seen its tail once, and if I hadn't, I would think Esther had an imaginary friend."

"I'm surprised I haven't seen her," said Rick. "Animals usually like me." He scanned the area around him as though expecting Pearl to pop up and surprise them. "Listen," he said to Curtis, "if you're serious about that offer to help, I would appreciate it. I could do it myself, but with two of us it'll be done in half the time, and then I can still help out Esther at the bistro."

"I'll come by for coffee in the morning before I go to the Shack. We can look at the back room then and decide what's needed."

"Great," said Rick, smiling. "I'm sure Esther will appreciate it."

"Are you talking about me?" asked Esther, stepping back into the hallway. "I heard my name."

"Just arranging to start on the shelves tomorrow," said Rick, lifting the bundle of bedding out of her arms.

"So soon?" she asked, looking relieved.

"Self-interest mainly," said Rick, winking at Curtis. "I'm less likely to stub my toes if these boxes are gone."

Curtis smiled to himself as he opened the door and held it for Esther to walk through. With Rick's help, finding ways to support Esther might be easier than he thought. He hoped she would appreciate it as much as he had appreciated her support for the past few years. Her friendship meant so much to him, and now that he was stronger, he needed to be a better friend.

But when they walked into the theater a few minutes later, Esther stopped to greet several people, and he found himself again on the sidelines of conversations. He wondered if he might not be the only one Esther kept a little at arm's length.

What did he need to do for her to let him in?

As they sat in the dark theater, the familiar scent of butter and salt enveloping them, Curtis found himself watching Esther more than the show. The light from the screen played across her face. She must have been keeping him at arm's length for years, and until today, he hadn't even noticed. He popped another few kernels of popcorn into his mouth, but the realization was what caught in his throat.

He stole another look at Esther, her expression rapt at the car chase unfolding on the screen. One hand hovered near her mouth, ready to cover her eyes if the action became too much—it was a habit he'd teased her about countless times. She was the same woman with whom he'd shared dozens of movies and yet, somehow, not the same woman at all. Or perhaps he was no longer the same man too blinded by his own pain to see her clearly.

Onscreen, a car exploded, and a moment later Esther yelped when the villain popped out of nowhere.

He chuckled and put his hand back into the popcorn bag.

"What's so funny?" she demanded, turning toward him.

"You are," he said. "I'm always surprised your popcorn doesn't end up in the seat behind us when we watch these movies."

"Are you saying I'm predictable?" she asked with mock severity.

"Anything but," he said, but he was lying. She was predictable in some ways. And he had come to rely on her for those.

She turned back to the movie, allowing him to continue watching her uninterrupted. He needed to get to know Esther better. To really understand her, not just as a reliable friend or a patient ear for his troubles, but as Esther, with her own needs and secrets and burdens.

What had changed?

Not Esther. She had always been the complex, self-contained person who gave so much while revealing so little. No, the change was in him. For the first time in four years, he was finally looking outward, beyond the narrow confines of his grief.

And what he saw both intrigued and unsettled him.

CHAPTER 5

The following morning, Esther woke to a pair of ice-blue eyes set in white fur, staring at her from inches away. Pearl's warm weight created a small dent in the blanket beside Esther's chest.

"Oh." Esther startled, her voice still thick with sleep. "Good morning."

She reached out and scratched the fluffy white Ragdoll behind the ears, feeling the familiar silky texture between her fingers. Six years of this same morning ritual, yet it still provided a comfort she couldn't quite explain. Pearl's rumbling purr vibrated against her fingertips as the cat leaned in to her touch. She was one of the few creatures who seemed to want

Esther purely for herself, and not for what she could provide.

After a moment of indulgence, Pearl dropped gracefully to the floor and padded toward the door. She paused with her tail held high like a question mark, turning to fix Esther with an expectant stare that needed no translation.

"Okay, okay." Esther sighed, swinging her legs over the side of the bed. The hardwood floor sent a chill through her bare feet. She padded over to open the door, her body moving on autopilot through the familiar morning choreography. "There you go. I'll get your breakfast in a few minutes."

Rick emerged from the guest bathroom, toweling off his hair. "I thought we could have breakfast in the bistro like the old days."

"I was talking to Pearl," said Esther.

"Pearl? Where is she?" Rick looked around the room, but the cat had slipped into one of her hiding spots.

"She'll come out when I feed her. Yes, I still have breakfast downstairs. I don't really have much food in the fridge up here anyway. I'll be ready in about fifteen minutes; just need to take a quick shower."

"No rush. I've been up since two—jet lag, I expect. I can wait another half hour."

After dressing and leaving food out for Pearl, who still hadn't poked her head out again, Esther and Rick went downstairs to start the baking.

"I had forgotten how peaceful it is to start the day early like this," he said. "And I love your commute to work."

"It's my favorite time of the day," said Esther, putting some flour into the big mixer. "It gives me time to think and relax after things are in the oven."

"Living alone seems to have its perks as well," said Rick. "Everything on your own schedule, and only things that you want in the house."

"I don't live completely alone. It helps to have Pearl. My cat keeps me company at night when I'm reading or working on my latest knitting project—though she does chase the yarn around sometimes."

"That could be annoying."

"I don't mind, really. Like I say, it's nice to have the company."

She turned on the mixer and added the rest of the ingredients for bread. When it was thoroughly mixed, she turned out the dough to a floured board and began to knead. She liked kneading the first few batches by hand. It helped reduce her stress levels in the morning.

"When she gets really annoying," said Esther, "I just practice my choir pieces. Pearl doesn't like my singing."

"You have a nice voice," said Rick, adding ingredients for the muffins he was making.

"Tell that to Pearl," said Esther. "She prefers to hide in my room until I finish."

"Maybe she just wants to wait to hear the final concert," joked Rick.

"Or she doesn't have my full attention, so she goes off to sulk."

Rick laughed. "She sounds like a very spoiled cat, sis."

"I suppose she is," said Esther. "But she is my fur baby."

"Well, I hope to meet her one of these days. We never had cats, or dogs. Dana hated them."

"They're a lot of work," said Esther. "And she did have a lot to do."

"Yes, and when the kids were young, I was away quite a bit on jobs. Still, I wish we'd given the boys a dog or cat to play with. They're nice additions to a family."

"Are you a dog person, then?"

"I like both, but right now I can't have either. First I have to find my son, and a home, and a job."

"When did you last hear from Cameron?"

"Last night. He texted me to ask me where I was staying."

"Did he say where he was?"

"No. Just said he was fine. Asked me where I was. That was it. And I know I sound like an old fart, but I really miss the old days when people would just pick up the phone and have a conversation. This texting stuff. Too much room for misinterpretation."

"Well," said Esther, as she put the dough into a large bowl to rise, "I guess you take him at his word. He's fine."

"I would, except I think Cameron would say that even if he was on an ice floe surrounded by sharks in the Caribbean Sea."

"Why would there be an ice floe in the Caribbean?" asked Esther, teasing him.

Rick looked up at her and grinned. "Okay, bad analogy, but you get my meaning. The kid never asks for help."

"He's been taught to be self-reliant."

"I suppose," said Rick. "But it would set my mind at ease if I could see him."

"When he wants you to visit, he'll be in touch. Meanwhile, all you can do is keep the lines of communication open."

"I'm just worried we'll end up like me and Dad," Rick said quietly, sharing a truth he clearly wasn't comfortable voicing.

Esther winced a little as she remembered the last time she had seen her brother and father together. What had started out as a difference in opinion had ended in a cold silence that still hadn't thawed, even after nearly ten years. Even when their father had a stroke, Rick had come only because she and their mother insisted they needed him. She remembered him standing at the doorway of their father's hospital room until she coaxed him to step forward and sit with them while their father slept. He had just begun to relax, and the energy in the room had shifted, when their father awakened, weak but with his steely gaze intact. He barely acknowledged Rick and asked only how the bistro was doing. He then demanded to know when he could leave because the business needed him.

Both men were as stubborn as the other, in her opinion.

But if Rick was back in town for a bit, maybe she could help them mend fences. Their family had lost too many years already to pride.

"Dad has mellowed a lot over the years since his stroke," she said carefully. "The doctor said he was lucky he got to the hospital when he did, and the stroke has made him realize he isn't immortal after all."

She turned to face her brother, noting how his hands —so like their father's—gripped the edge of the counter. "You could try reaching out to him. Be the bigger man." She offered a soft smile. "He's not likely to be the first to reach out."

"No, he's not, is he?" Rick spooned the batter into the muffin tins, placed the tins into the oven, and set the timer. "What else do we need to do before we can eat? I'm starved."

"I'm going to start on the scones first. But you could make the breakfast. The grill should be warm enough now."

"Omelettes okay?" he asked, opening the walk-in freezer.

"Perfect." Her mouth was already watering. Rick made the best omelettes.

He came out of the freezer with a bowl of ingredients and started on his task. "When do Mom and Dad get back?" he asked as he cracked the eggs.

"The first week of June."

"What do they do about the house while they're

away?" He picked up a whisk to beat the eggs and added a touch of milk.

"This year they got a house sitter. Usually I go up and look in on the house, but this year they told me not to bother. I was busy enough with the shortage of staff. I guess they decided I didn't need the extra bother." She turned out the dough for scones, shaped it, and cut it into equal wedges.

"That was probably Mom's idea," said Rick.

"Maybe, but Dad agreed. As I say, he's mellowing."

"Just hope the house sitter doesn't scratch anything. Dad will have a cow."

"You do know how to hold a grudge, don't you?"

He poured the eggs onto the grill and used the spatula to shape the mixture into a circle, adding the other ingredients on top. "I will admit I got into a bit of a fender bender with his car…"

"His *new* car," said Esther.

"Okay, his *new* car," corrected Rick. "But I got it fixed, paid for the repairs, and all he could say was that I was irresponsible."

"He wasn't really himself that day. He bought the car just before he had that heart surgery. He hadn't had a chance to really drive it, and then—"

"I realize that, but he never even asked me how I was doing. Do you know I had to have physio for a year to get over that whiplash? He didn't even want to admit that I didn't cause the accident."

"He's not always reasonable," said Esther. "And I'm sorry he didn't handle it well. And I'm glad you didn't get hurt worse than you did."

"Thanks, but that's not the point. You and Mom were there for me. Dad not so much."

"I know. He's all about tough love, which only works on certain people."

"I don't know how you can defend him. Look what he did to you. He didn't even want to help you get out."

Esther thought of those first few years of marriage and quickly shoved the memory aside. It had taken her a few years of therapy to get through that time in her life, and she didn't like to revisit it. Instead of answering him, she asked, "How are the eggs doing?"

"What? Crap!" He spun back to the grill and lifted the lids off the omelettes. Using the spatula, he flipped them over. "Just about done." He went to the side-board that held the toaster. "Rye, sourdough, or white?"

"Sourdough, please," she said putting the scones into the oven and setting the timer.

"Don't think I've forgotten my question," said Rick, as he scooped up the omelettes one by one with his spatula and slid them onto plates. "How did you forgive him?"

She took out two cups and poured them coffee. "You still like cream and sugar?"

"Yes, one sugar, two cream."

She took the cream out of a small condiment fridge she kept near the front of the kitchen and added it to the cups. Then she picked them up, along with two forks and two knives, and joined him at the little table set up for staff breaks.

"Well?" he asked.

She blew out a breath. "I figured out that if I forgave him, I would no longer have to spend a lot of energy on it. I can't change Dad or the past. All I can do is change my reaction to him. And so I chose not to spend any more time resenting him. Living in the same town, with Mom helping me during the summer, I couldn't really cut him out of my life like you did." She sat down and picked up her coffee.

"You think that's what I did?"

"Didn't you?" The buzzer on the oven went off. She sighed, put her cup down without taking a sip, and went to the oven to remove the piping-hot muffins.

"Is that what he thinks?" asked Rick from his seat at the table.

"What are we supposed to think? You don't even reach out to me except for the occasional text on my birthday." Esther set the hot muffins aside to cool and loaded another two tins Rick had prepared into the oven.

Rick didn't answer for a while. "I'm sorry, Esther."

"Thanks, but it's not me you need to apologize to. You and I are good. What I don't understand is why."

"It was easier not to. You know how Dana is. She didn't like Dad. Or anyone outside her immediate friend group, really. She wanted me to spend time with her, to help her with her mother until she died last year, and then there were the boys. Helping Sean get set up in the business and helping Cameron get through school and figure out his future—though that is still a work in progress—took a lot of time. Before I knew it, a year passed, then another, and soon I lost touch, even if I didn't intend to. The pandemic didn't help."

"I know how easy it is to become alienated from your family. I was married to Seth, remember?" She rubbed her left arm, though the physical pain from the injuries she'd sustained was long gone.

"I think that was a bit different," he said, reaching out to pat her arm. "He was isolating you from everyone intentionally. Dana didn't really do that."

"Didn't she?" Esther said softly.

Esther had spent three years in therapy. working through exactly how her ex had managed to become her whole world—how he'd methodically shrunk it until he was the only person she saw or interacted with. First it was "I miss you when you're gone" and "Wouldn't you rather stay home with me?" Then it became checking her phone, timing her grocery trips, questioning friendships, until it was easier to let them go than to face his suspicions.

She couldn't see the difference between Seth and Dana except that Dana, as far as she knew, had never broken any of Rick's bones or put him in the hospital after a beating. But isolation was isolation.

"She just liked to be the center of attention and was invested in building her business. She needed me to be there full-on. I think you, and Mom and Dad, were just cut off because of circumstance."

Esther didn't agree but didn't want to argue. "Well, you're here now, and that's what's important. I'm sure Mom and Dad will be glad to see you when they get home."

"Maybe," he said, his face unreadable.

"Dad really is mellowing out. I think that stroke scared him. He's been reevaluating his life, volunteering, and taking time to spend with Mom. Like real, quality time. You know?"

"That would be a switch. I don't know why she stayed with him so long."

"Because she loves him," said Esther. "And she wasn't any easier to live with, you know. Dad put pressure on you, and Mom put pressure on me. It's why I got married so young. I needed an escape."

"I guess we were both trying to get away, which makes it ironic that we are here in this kitchen all these years later, baking and getting ready to open."

She laughed. "Yes, it is ironic. If only we had known we'd be here all these years later, maybe we wouldn't have tried so hard to leave."

His laugh sounded forced. Where was her jovial brother? And how would she get him back? Maybe if she could help find Cameron, and he found work, it would help.

"Do you really have any idea where Cameron is?"

He filled his fork with a bite of food and shook off her question. "Why don't you tell me about this Curtis guy? How long have you been dating?" he picked up his fork and took a bite.

"We aren't dating," she said. "We're friends."

Rick shook his head and grabbed his coffee, studying her over the rim of the mug. His eyes—too observant, too familiar with her tells—held a knowing gleam that made her want to leave. "Are you sure about that? Because I'm pretty sure that guy is into you."

"He's in grief," she said firmly. "He's still getting over Maggie, his late wife."

The timer bell sounded then—a rescue she gratefully accepted. She busied herself removing another batch of scones from the oven, keeping her back to Rick as the flush crept up her neck. Why did he keep making assumptions about Curtis? And why did it bother her so much?

Because in the dead of night, when she was lying awake staring at the ceiling with Pearl curled against her side, she sometimes wished she had someone other than her cat to talk to. Someone who would listen to her challenges at the café, give her ideas about how to handle situations that arose during the business association meetings, make her laugh, or just lie there beside her, reading a book in companionable silence. And when she thought about who she wanted that someone to be, it was always Curtis who came to mind: his kind eyes, his calm way of walking in the world, the way he made her feel safe.

But that was only on those few occasions when she wasn't sleeping, she told herself. When she needed an opinion rather than Pearl's friendly meow of agreement. Even if those occasions were much more frequent lately.

She turned to her cooled scones and arranged them on the tray she would soon slide into the showcase beneath the counter. She placed them in even lines, ensuring they were perfectly uniform. She liked this small task. It was something that she could control.

Rick rose and followed her back to the oven, forcing her to look at him. "So you're telling me you never thought about him differently than that?"

"No, of course not," she shot back. But she didn't turn to face him. She didn't want to admit that his words had hit a nerve.

"Right, if you say so." Rick shrugged and walked over to pour himself another cup of coffee.

She knew from his tone that he didn't believe her. And she didn't blame him, because she was outright lying. Of course she was interested in Curtis, but he was still in love with his wife, and she didn't want to even whisper the possibility of changing their relationship. Their real, reliable friendship was too precious to risk on something as transient and unpredictable as romance.

So instead she had to keep him firmly in the friend category, and that meant not getting too close, because she would only break her heart and lose a friend she wanted to keep at all costs.

"Thanks for the help this morning," she said, after she'd set new batches of muffins and cinnamon buns in the oven and returned to her meal. She was determined to change the subject. "And for making breakfast. It looks great."

"Most important meal of the day," he said in the same way their mother used to say it.

"Yes, though I admit I often skip it these days," said Esther. "Coffee and a bit of toast with avocado usually get me through until lunchtime."

"Happy to help until I figure out what I'll be doing next," said Rick as he took a bite, a shadow darkening his face.

"I'm sure you'll find Cameron soon," said Esther with a half smile. "If Sean told him you don't share Dana's opinion, I'm sure he'll be in touch again soon."

"I hope so. Just wish I knew that he was okay."

"Do you have a recent picture of him? I haven't seen him since he was—what? Twelve, thirteen?"

"Really? I'm sorry. I have been a poor brother, haven't I?" He fished out his phone from his pocket and scrolled through his pictures. "Here's one from about a year ago. The last time we were together."

Esther took the phone and peered at her nephew, whom she hadn't set eyes on in years. The young man looking at her from the screen looked familiar. She had seen him recently. But where?

"What's wrong?" asked Rick.

She looked up at her brother. "He's here, Rick. I saw Cameron when I was at a meeting at the hotel a couple of weeks ago. He was helping with the audio."

"Are you sure?"

"I didn't recognize him. Even if I had seen him recently, I wouldn't have expected to see him here."

"He's here?" Rick said softly. "And working?"

"As far as I could tell, yes."

"Esther, you have just made my day. Now all I have to do is find him." He rose, excited, as though he were going to go off that moment to hunt down his son.

Esther reached out and pulled at his shirt hem. "Sit down," she said. "You can't go off half-cocked."

"But he's here," he said, sinking back into the chair.

"Think about it," said Esther. "He's reached out. He knows where you are. You've opened the door for him to come in. Forcing him before he's ready will just set him off again."

"I can't just do nothing," said Rick.

"You can stay here, be available, and send him a text every day or so to let him know you are thinking of him. The fact that he came to the town where you grew up, where he had some good times as a kid, that must mean something." She watched his jaw tighten as he thought through what she was saying.

Finally, he nodded. "Okay, I'll do it your way," he said. "I'll give him a few days. But if I haven't heard anything soon, I'm going to start making inquiries."

"That seems fair. I'll even help search," said Esther, rising and walking over to the coffee machine. "Meanwhile, do you want another coffee before we open the door?"

"Sure," he said. "That would be great."

She poured him a fresh cup and noticed that a spark of hope had come back to his eyes—and, with it, a hint of the old Rick. And for that she was grateful.

CHAPTER 6

*R*ick worked steadily through the breakfast rush, the clink of silverware and murmur of conversations washing over him like familiar music. At nine thirty, when the traffic had dwindled to the occasional late-morning customer, the bell above the door announced Soo Yin, Esther's regular Wednesday help. Her arrival brought a burst of cool spring air and the faint scent of cherry blossoms from the tree outside.

Esther smiled and welcomed the young woman, and once Soo Yin had put away her belongings, Esther smoothly and confidently discussed with her and Nova what needed to be done. They set to work.

Rick watched his sister as she moved with purpose to the kitchen. This wasn't the same girl who used to jump at loud noises and second-guess herself about even the simplest decisions. She had grown into a confident woman, and the business seemed to be running well.

Once she returned to the kitchen, she moved some dirty dishes away from the counter and into a nearby bin before walking over to join him. "I think you and I can take a break now," she said. "Come, and I'll show you the storage room."

He nodded, folded the apron he had been wearing, and tossed it into a bin for washing. "You've got a great system here, Esther."

"Thanks," she said. "I had to modernize once Dad finally relinquished control and agreed to sell the business to me. You know how he was."

"You don't have to remind me." He grimaced and turned toward the hall. "And the remodel is great. It looks like a modern city café." He glanced around appreciatively at the sage-green walls, polished floors, and shelves tastefully decorated with pottery and books.

"I decided to do that when they were away in Mexico a few years ago." Esther laughed, falling into step beside him.

"Good call. I would have waited until they left too," said Rick. "What did Dad think of it?"

"Oh, you know how he is. He grumbled about the waste of money, but when he saw how many new customers came in, well, he decided it wasn't such a bad idea after all." Esther chuckled as she pushed open the door of the storage room. The musty smell that escaped nearly overpowered them.

"We need to open a window," said Rick, pushing past her and walking to the little window high up near the back of the store. He pulled over a step stool climbed up to slide open the glass. "You finally replaced this old thing," said Rick, motioning to the window. "It used to stick all the time."

"Yes, when you left and I took over stock duty, I kept bugging Dad to come and open it when I was in here. I guess he got tired of me bugging him, so he finally replaced it."

"The bars are the same, though," said Rick.

"I never knew why we needed them, but you know Dad. Always worried about a break-in. And now I don't dare get them removed just in case he's right and someone wiggles their way in here one day."

"I used to have a love–hate relationship with this room," said Rick, stepping back down. "It was a prison, but at the same time it gave me an excuse to get away from Dad's constant scrutiny."

"You did spend a lot of time in here," said Esther. "I used to envy you because I got stuck on dishwashing and kitchen duty."

"I'm sorry. I never realized you hated it so much." He looked around the tiny room. "I remember this place being bigger."

"You were smaller," said Esther, walking over to one of the two walls of shelving. "I thought we could add a few shelves here, at the bottom," she said, pointing to a spot near the shelving unit that went from the ceiling to halfway down the wall. "Dad always used to just stack boxes here, but they should be on a platform. Not a big one. Just six to ten centimeters off the ground. Enough to keep the boxes off the floor while still leaving room to stack the big ones."

"Anything else you want to change while we're in here?" he asked. "We could rebuild some of these others. This one, for example, is really old." He shoved at one of the shelving slats, and it shifted easily.

"That's a lot of work," she said. "It can wait a few years."

"Or I can do it now," said Rick. "Curtis has offered to help, and it would probably only take us a couple of days."

"He has other things to do besides help me," said Esther looking at the floor and up at the shelves as though considering his offer.

"I think he would like to help you," said Rick.

"Maybe if he has a crew that needs work," she said. "I know he has a few kids working with him this semester."

"Kids? I thought he worked with older guys."

"He and a few of the men at the Men's Shack have become mentors to kids interested in trades careers. He's teaching them skills, how to work on a jobsite, that kind of thing."

"He sounds part saint," laughed Rick.

"What?" Esther swiveled to look at him. "Why would you say that?"

"The way you talk about him, it sounds like the man can do no wrong."

"He does give a lot back to the community," said Esther, a note of pride in her voice.

"A man after your own heart," teased Rick.

"Nothing wrong with wanting to help your neighbors, Rick." She looked at him sternly, but he noticed her faint blush.

He bit back a grin. "Nope, nothing wrong with that. Speaking of Curtis, he should be here soon."

"He's probably having coffee," she said. "He usually comes in around now."

"During the slow time?" he said. "That makes sense."

"What's that supposed to mean?"

"Nothing," said Rick, but he waggled his eyebrows again. "Now tell me about this space here." He pointed to a relatively empty wall. "Is there something you want to use it for?"

"It used to hold that old desk," she said.

"The one where I did my homework," he said. "You finally got rid of it."

"That was Dad. After you left, he decided I had to do my homework at one of the tables out front. It was like he blamed the desk for you leaving."

"He was the one that made me leave," muttered Rick. "His constant harping about how I needed to take over the business."

"I know. But, like I said, he's mellowed," said Esther.

Rick looked away, focusing on a crack in the wall. "Maybe. Or maybe you're just accustomed to it." The old hurt still felt fresh, like a bruise that could never quite heal. Even now, at fifty-two, he could remember that eighteen-year-old boy desperate to escape his father's plans for his life.

"He'll be back in a few weeks, and you can decide for yourself," said Esther, cutting the conversation short. "I should get back to the front. I'll send Curtis back here when he arrives."

Rick walked over to the window, where warm sunshine and birdsong from a nearby tree were finding their way through the bars. Far in the distance, he could hear children playing.

When he was younger, he had longed to join the children outside, but from the time he was ten until he was fourteen, he had been forced to come here after school and most weekends to supervise Esther's homework and pitch in with the never-ending chores the restaurant business required.

Thankfully, when Esther turned twelve, she started wheedling about being allowed to take music lessons. Like a drop of water on a stone, she finally wore down her mother's defenses, citing how good it would be to sing Italian arias, and Canadian music like her heroines Celine Dion and Anne Murray.

Their mother, a huge fan of Italian opera—and a woman who knew how to get around her husband—helped convince their father that Esther should be able to try. And, after what must have been months of cajoling, their dad had finally relented.

That had opened the door for him to ask to play a sport like the rest of the boys. Though he desperately wanted to play hockey, he knew that was a nonstarter. The practices were too early, the equipment and ice time too expensive, and the arenas colder than a walk-in fridge. But soccer… well, that was a sport his father knew, a sport he had played when he was a child with his older brother, a sport he was happy to support.

The next two years had been easier. He and his father bonded over the game, and his dad even took time out to play in the evenings and show him some skills.

Unfortunately, the loosening of tension between him and his father hadn't lasted, not once Rick turned sixteen and took his first shop class at school. His passion for soccer was soon matched by his passion for building things with his hands. This passion gained him recognition from his teacher, Mr. Zegler, who saw his potential and encouraged him to take a trade.

A trade that would soon take him away from the bakery, his family, and Sunshine Bay.

His father had never forgiven him.

Rick still had soccer, and he had his sister and his mother to thank for that. It had helped him bond with boys at school and feel included for the first time in his young life. And later, it helped him bond with his sons, who both took up the game. Even now, when he could, he played the occasional pickup game with men he had known for years. At least he had until recently. He would have to ask Esther if she knew of any beer leagues.

He walked over to the other shelves, tested their stability, and decided that the whole lot needed to be pulled out. They were old, and many were weakened. Besides, the room could really use a new coat of paint.

Footsteps approached, and he turned to find Curtis in the doorway.

"Thanks for coming," he said, walking over to shake Curtis's hand.

"Glad to help. Esther is always helping me out. It's the least I can do."

"Really?" asked Rick, hoping to hear a little more about his sister from another's point of view.

"Esther is one of a kind, as you know," said Curtis. "She provides baked goods for our concerts, a space for us to meet in the evening, and she's even taken on

the role of president of the downtown business association."

"That must keep her busy." Esther hadn't mentioned
any of this to him.

"Yes, she's always doing little things to help others. I
don't know where she finds the time, really."

"She has always been driven and organized," said
Rick, "and she could convince a fish to give up
water."

Curtis laughed. "I suppose she could at that. Now,
show me what it is we need to do. I have a discount at
the local building store if I use some of my crew to
help."

"Your crew?"

"Actually, I have a couple of crews. But the one I'm
thinking of is a small band of teenagers looking for
work experience. This is a small enough project that I
could get three or four of them involved. They get
work experience. We get cheap labor."

"I'm sure we can pay them."

"Yes, I usually try to get them some wages through

one of the grants I apply for, but it's minimal compared to what a ticketed worker would cost."

Over the next hour, they discussed the details of the plan, measured the room, and identified the required materials. "I have to go to the store today anyway, so I'll order these," said Curtis. "I should be able to pick it all up tomorrow morning, and bring in the helpers at about two—they get some time off school when they are involved in a project."

"Great," said Rick. "I can start disassembling this, and we can begin tomorrow after the lunch rush."

"We should ask Esther if she has any of the paint left from the front. Or at least a paint swatch so we can match it."

"It's a storeroom," said Rick. "No need to get fancy."

"No, but Esther might have something to say about it. I think we should ask."

"Sure," said Rick, shrugging. "You go ahead." He smiled to himself as he watched Curtis head down the hall toward Esther. "Any excuse to talk to my sister," he mumbled, shaking his head.

He climbed back up to close the window and noticed his T-shirt was streaked with dust. He would need to change before going back to the restaurant to help with the afternoon shift.

Upstairs at Esther's apartment, he pushed open the door and stepped past the boxes to his room. A white streak flashed past him when he bent over to get a clean shirt from his suitcase.

"Hey," he said to the spot where he'd last seen Pearl. "I'm not going to hurt you."

But the cat was hovering just out of sight. Waiting and watching.

There and not there.

Just like his son Cameron.

Well, he was determined to win them both over in the coming days. But Esther's shelves wouldn't build themselves, and he needed something to keep busy. He washed and dressed, then left the apartment, careful not to let Pearl escape as he closed the door. He needn't have worried. She never emerged again.

As he clattered back down the stairs, he found himself smiling.

Yesterday he had arrived with a sense of despair, and with no plan except to find his son. Today he had a job to keep him busy, a renewed relationship with his sister, a new acquaintance in Curtis, and hope that his son was just as close to him as the elusive Pearl.

All he had to do was learn a little patience.

CHAPTER 7

Curtis walked into the bistro just after two the next day, trailed by a trio of teens from the local high school. He instinctively glanced at the counter, searching for Esther, but found only two of her staff wiping down tables and restocking shelves.

Disappointed, he turned toward the back of the bistro. Esther had to be in the kitchen, her favorite place, getting ready for the evening. They wouldn't be closing until nine tonight, so he had to make sure the crew kept the noise down.

Ideally, they would be doing this after business hours, but schedules hadn't allowed for that.

Rick was in the storeroom, and, as promised, he was already disassembling the old shelves.

"You have a lot done," he said, looking at the pile of old shelving set in the corner.

"I'm glad I decided to go down to the bones," said Rick. "These things aren't very sturdy anymore." He held up a piece of wood that had snapped in two when he removed it.

"Do you have a place to put this?" Curtis gestured to the pile. "I can get this lot to help us with that."

Rick turned around to see the others who had trailed into the room.

"Rick, this is Symone. She's a grade twelve student and has been working on a few jobs with me since… when?" He looked at a Symone.

"Two years," she said.

"That long, eh?"

Symone looked like she was refraining from rolling her eyes, and he sighed inwardly. No matter how long he worked with her, he could not get her to speak any more than necessary.

"Symone, this is Rick." Symone forced her chin up in acknowledgement and reached forward to shake Rick's proffered hand. Then, to Curtis's surprise, she added, "This is Deacon, and that's Miles." She pointed to the two young men, who also shook Rick's hand. Maybe some of what he'd been telling her about customer relations was sinking in after all.

"Deacon and Miles are in grade ten," Rick added. "This is their second job, but they're hard workers."

"Where do you want this stuff?" asked Symone, and Rick led them out to the back of the store and showed them a large garbage skiff they could use. Symone gave instructions to the other pair, and soon the three of them had cleared out the old shelving leaving the room empty.

"Got a broom?" asked Symone.

"There are two in the cupboard just across the hall," said Rick. Within minutes, Miles and Deacon had swept the room clean, while Curtis moved his truck to the back of the store and Symone helped him bring in the paint and painting supplies.

Two hours later, the walls had been filled, sanded and

painted with two coats of fresh paint that brightened up the room considerably.

"Great work," said Rick when they were done putting away the paint and tools. "You must be thirsty. Let's grab a snack before you leave."

The trio smiled—whether at the praise or the offer of food, Curtis wasn't sure.

When they entered the bistro, they took a table near the back. Rick placed their orders and came back with a couple of glasses of pop, a latte, and two coffees. He spent the next half hour asking the trio about their plans and letting them know what the job would require the next day.

"We'll start off at the Shack," said Curtis. "We can cut all the boards there and then just bring them here to be assembled."

"That's a good idea," said Rick. "I can meet you there."

Curtis took a card out of his wallet and handed it to Rick. As he did, he glanced over at the counter and saw Esther watching him.

"Jack already gave me a card," said Rick.

"This one has my direct number," said Curtis, dragging his eyes away from Esther and back to Rick. "In case something comes up."

"Right," said Rick, taking the card. "Thanks."

"No problem," said Curtis, his eyes straying back in Esther's direction. She smiled at him, and he smiled in return as she walked toward them with a plate of baked goods.

"Here's something to go with your coffees," she said, placing it on the table. "The paint looks nice. I wasn't convinced that I needed new paint, but it does make the room look more welcoming, doesn't it?"

"I agree," said Rick. "And tomorrow we're going to be cutting boards at the Shack."

"Nice," said Esther, smiling again at Curtis before turning to Rick. "I'm sure you'll like the Shack. It's got a lot of great equipment."

She left them to their food and drinks, talked a moment to her staff, then disappeared into the back room again. leaving Curtis a little sad. Esther always made the room brighter when she was in it.

But at least he was able to help her. And if he could help her brother get connected and find a job, that would help her even more.

CHAPTER 8

The following day, Esther was pleased to discover all her staff were healthy again, which meant that she could leave the bistro for a couple of hours. So when Rick borrowed her car to go to the Shack a few kilometers away, she took her opportunity to leave too.

She headed straight to the place where she had last seen Cameron.

The Sunshine Bay Hotel, a weathered brick building nestled among manicured gardens, stood proudly at the end of the main street. Hostas with bright spring leaves lined the low-maintenance garden beds, while hanging baskets—already heavy with verbena, creeping jenny, begonias, and a variety of other flowers Esther couldn't name—adorned both sides of the entrance.

Guests could enjoy meals in the hotel's restaurant, which offered a perfect view of the bay. The sailboats were already out in full force. The hotel, perched on a rise and known for its charm, attracted both tourists and locals seeking a special experience. With a spa on site and a newly refurbished restaurant run by an award-winning chef, it had become a favored destination for those wanting a taste of indulgence in Sunshine Bay.

Esther visited the hotel only for special occasions like a friend's recent fiftieth birthday and her parents' wedding anniversary. But now that Spencer Bingham, the new owner, had taken the reins, the hotel also hosted the regular quarterly meetings of the downtown business association.

Though she was now a more regular visitor, she still found, when she stepped into the foyer, that the space radiated welcome. No, it was more than that. It was a promise that whoever came here would be taken care of.

She was glad it was part of her community and that Spencer Bingham had decided to make the hotel his special project. She also appreciated that he had opened the doors to the business community—though she expected his discounts paid off tenfold, because many business owners entertained or referred clients here now.

Esther walked up to the desk to see if Spencer was available, and she was greeted by a familiar smile.

"Hello, Brooke, how are you today?"

The young woman, who had worked for Esther for several summers before landing a job in the hotel two months prior, was dressed in a smart blue suit and brilliant white blouse, her hair swept up in an elegant bun. "Hello, Esther," she said brightly.

"I see you have a new job. Weren't you with the catering staff last time I was here?"

"Yes, but when I asked if I could do a practicum at the front desk as part of my tourism diploma, they let me try."

"Are you enjoying it?"

"I love it." She leaned closer to Esther. "And I need to thank you for all you taught me about customer service. Your advice has helped me get through some sticky situations."

Esther laughed. "All I taught you was good conflict resolution skills, but I'm glad it helped."

"Speaking of help, is there something I can do for you?"

"I was going to ask Spencer, but you might know. I'm looking for a young man who works for the audio company that the hotel contracts with. Do you happen to know which company is being used?"

"Umm…" Brooke hesitated for a moment as though considering whether to speak.

Esther decided to wait a moment, but when Brooke hadn't answered by the time she counted to ten, she said, "I can find Spencer and ask him. He'll know. Sorry to bother you."

"No. Wait. Do you mean Cameron?"

"Why yes, I do. Do you know where I can find him?" Esther asked, trying to keep her voice casual.

"Umm…" Hesitation again. Brooke glanced down the hall and then back at Esther. There was something there. A caring, a concern. Brooke was protecting Cameron.

"Is he here, perhaps?"

"He's a good person, you know," Brooke said suddenly. "He doesn't talk much about his family, but when he does…" She stopped herself, clearly uncertain about how much to share.

"I'm not here to cause problems," Esther said softly. "His father—my brother—is in town. They haven't spoken in a while."

Brooke looked miserable for a moment. "Why don't I go see if he's available." She turned toward the other woman working at the counter and said she would be right back.

"Okay," said Esther, waiting while Brooke walked down the hall, heels clicking on the smooth marble that led to the large meeting room that the business community usually used.

Ten minutes later she returned, looking chagrined. "Um. He's pretty busy at the moment. Do you think I could give him a message?"

Esther had considered that she might not see Cameron today. In fact, she had visions of having to track him down somewhere else later that week. Her intention was only to get the business name where he worked and to call him. But what to say?

"Could you tell him that his aunt was here to see him?"

"Sure, I can tell him," she said.

"He doesn't know me very well," Esther added quickly, feeling the sudden need to explain why she and her nephew weren't in contact. "I haven't seen him since he was about twelve. Well, that's not entirely true. I saw him last month when he ran audio for our meeting, but I didn't recognize him. If I hadn't seen a recent picture, I still wouldn't realize who he was." Now she was overexplaining, but she got the feeling that Brooke knew Cameron better than she let on. Perhaps well enough to help her bring Cameron and Rick together.

"I'll tell him," said Brooke, looking a little less guarded now. "Really."

"Could you also ask him to call me? Or drop by the

bistro? I have someone staying with me who would love to see him."

"Yes," said Brooke. "I'll let him know. Don't worry."

Esther wanted to ask more. How is he? What's he like? But she had already shared far more than she was comfortable sharing. So she thanked Brooke and turned to leave, tucking away the knowledge that Cameron was known to Brooke and that Brooke might be able to help.

She wouldn't pressure the girl to pressure Cameron, but it was nice to know her nephew had made a friend. A nice one at that.

Back at the bistro, she was in the kitchen preparing some food for the evening when Rick returned and popped his head into the kitchen.

"We've got all the wood cut," he said, looking tired but pleased. "We'll put it into the back, and then tomorrow afternoon we should be able to get most of the work finished. Do you mind putting together another snack tray for them? They've been working hard, and I think they enjoyed it yesterday."

"Consider it done," said Esther. "I'll be out in a few

minutes with some grub. Just ask Nova for the drinks and let her know I'll pay for it on our tab."

"Thanks, Esther," he said, and she got to work putting together one tray of hummus and vegetables and one tray of sandwiches, muffins, and scones. They had cleared the plate the day before.

When she walked out to the seating area, she found the crew happily chatting and sipping on their drinks. Rick was in the middle of the group, entertaining them with a story of derring-do from his time working as an electrician on a high-rise site. She placed the platter in the middle of the table and grabbed small plates for each of them, all the while feeling like she was being watched. When she turned, she found Curtis standing in the hallway, observing the crew. She set down the plates, napkins, and cutlery and walked over to him.

"You don't want to join them?" she asked.

"Oh, I will," he said. "I was just watching how your brother interacts with them. They've been learning a lot from him today."

"Feeling a little left out?" she asked, giving him a

little tap on his shoulder to show that she was teasing him.

He looked down at her and smiled warmly. "No, I was wondering if he would consider coming to work with me for a while—you know, until he finds a better job. The kids have really taken to him. Even Symone, who barely speaks when she's around me."

"Well, he has trained his share of workers over the years."

"Do you think he would consider it? It wouldn't pay much. I do have some promising contracts coming up, though, so things could get better."

She looked at her brother, who had finished his story and was now listening to one of the others. Miles? Or maybe it was Deacon. "Do you want me to ask him?"

"Nah, I'll ask him. I was just wondering if you might know."

"I haven't seen my brother in several years, Curtis. He and I were close when I was young, and he's helped me out when I needed it, but your guess is as good as mine on this. Though he does look like he's enjoying himself."

"Well, I'll take that as a sign and ask him once we are done with this project. I was wondering if he would be interested in helping with the bat boxes. Jack can't help much because Sylvia's sister isn't well. She has to have some surgery, so Jack has to leave for a bit."

"He mentioned the bat boxes, said he might come by and help," she said, laughing. She never expected Rick to know about bat boxes, but he had surprised her. Maybe this would be a good job for him.

"Good," said Curtis, looking back up at Rick. "It might help him meet people at least."

"Yes," said Esther. "And it would give him something to do for a few weeks until he decides whether he'll stay or not."

"Do you think he won't?" he asked.

"Depends on what happens with his son, I think," said Esther.

"His son?"

"It's not my story to tell," she said. "But I'll tell you later if he's okay with me sharing."

"I understand," said Curtis, though she could tell by his tone that he didn't. But what did he expect? She wouldn't want Rick to tell anyone about her private life either. It was a small town, and for now they both had to live here.

Curtis excused himself to join the crew, and Esther shivered in the suddenly cool air. She looked to the front door, but it was firmly closed. The chill wasn't coming from that direction.

CHAPTER 9

Rick and Curtis stayed back talking after the crew had finished their coffees and left for the day.

"They are a hardworking bunch," said Rick. "And quick learners. I think that younger one, Deacon, has the makings of a craftsman when it comes to working with wood."

"He does give attention to detail." Curtis smiled. "And he's eager to learn."

"He showed me the chair legs he's making there at the Shack. Nice work."

"His grandfather owned a furniture store a few years back, and I think he showed Deacon how to use a lathe. It's actually his grandfather's old lathe that we have now. His grandfather works mainly on smaller items like bowls. Says the larger stuff isn't what he's interested in anymore." It never failed to please Curtis to see how generous people—mostly older men—were with their time and tools and knowledge.

"Well, if that skill is genetic, then the kid's got the gene," said Rick.

"I've been pleased to see Symone come out of her shell this week too," said Curtis. thinking that maybe now was the time to brooch the subject of Rick working with him.

"She'll be a good asset to any job site. She's a leader, and very safety conscious."

"Yes, and I've appreciated you giving them all so much patience. It's helped them get exposure to a different work style. I'm hoping to give them several opportunities to learn from people other than me during the program."

"You must enjoy your job," said Rick.

"Most of the time, yes. Though when you work with people, there are always unexpected challenges."

"I know what you mean. When I was running my business, I thought training new employees was one of the fun parts of my job. There were a few who gave me some gray hair, but for the most part they seemed to like building things or solving problems."

"The people part is the fun part," said Curtis. "What I find most tiring is always having to find new funding and constantly applying for grants."

"Writing not your favorite thing?"

"It's interesting, and I enjoy working with the community to find new projects, but you have to then be aware of where to get the funding and how to approach the sponsors. I'm getting better at it, but there's always something to learn."

"Just like being in business," said Rick. "New suppliers, new materials, new customers. It's part of the fun, though. Never a dull moment."

Curtis laughed. "When you put it that way, I suppose you're right."

"But you like it?" asked Rick, and Curtis looked at him sharply. It felt like more than just an idle question.

"I do. I've been doing this for nearly ten years, and we've helped a lot of men—and the men have really helped me." He rubbed his hands along the surface of the table, smoothing away rough patches that weren't there. "Especially when Maggie was going through chemo and then palliative care."

"How long ago did you lose her?" Rick asked softly.

Curtis looked up. "It's been four years. Four long years." His eyes flickered from Rick's intense gaze back to the table. "I think I was in shock for part of that time. Stuck on autopilot—watching someone else live my life. I coped by helping my sons through their loss. The more I helped them and others, the less I had to think about my own grief." He smiled faintly, remembering. "Anthony moved back home once he finished the first year of his diploma. Logan was still in high school. They both took it so differently. Anthony got angry at the world; Logan just went silent for months, studied harder than ever, focused on getting the grades so he could go to med school to carry forward his mother's legacy. Esther listened." His gaze strayed to the counter, where she was helping a customer, before he forced it back to the table. "And the men at the Shack… they understood without me having to explain. Some had been through similar losses themselves."

"It would be good to speak to others who have had the experience," said Rick. "When you change your whole life, it can be lonely."

"Yes, yes, it can," said Curtis, looking up at Rick again. The pain was there in his eyes, and it was clear that Rick was struggling with something.

They sat for a while in silence, each lost in his own thoughts. Then Rick looked up at Curtis again.

"Can anyone join the Shack?" he asked.

"Well, the members are technically men over fifty, but others come in to get help with their projects." Curtis leaned forward. "And I have the student mentor project, of course. We take on small side jobs to give them work experience."

"I'd like to find out more," said Rick. "Maybe learn a bit of wood turning."

"Sure," said Curtis. "Why don't you come over again later this week?" He looked Rick in the eye. "If you've enjoyed working with this gang, I could use an extra pair of hands for the next couple of months and not everyone is comfortable with teenagers."

"Depends on the teenager," mumbled Rick. He either wasn't taking the hint that Curtis was trying to offer him a job or was deliberately avoiding the topic.

"Well, not all kids click," said Curtis.

"Especially when they're your own," said Rick.

Curtis noticed Esther watching them. Was she angry? Curious? He decided to ignore her and focus on Rick instead. He needed to get to know him more before he tried to get him to help out at the Shack. Rick was hurting, and Curtis needed to listen.

"How many kids do you have?" asked Curtis.

"Two," said Rick, looking at his empty coffee cup and then back up at Curtis. "I have two boys. Sean, my eldest, is in Ontario, running the business he and I set up together. My youngest is here."

"Here?" Curtis was surprised. "Esther never mentioned that her nephew was living in Sunshine Bay."

"We just found out he's here. Working in audio, I believe, though we aren't exactly sure where."

"Audio?" Rick's mind raced. "Maybe I know him. Or my son does."

"Your son?"

"A couple of friends and I have a band. Both my boys play in it when Logan is in town. Anthony, my eldest, runs the audio for us. He's also working for a company that gets subcontracted when they put on shows at the arts center, or when there's a film crew that needed local help. What's your son's name?"

"Cameron."

"Long dark hair? Tattoo of a bird on his wrist?

"Yes." Rick's eyes lit up. "You know him?"

"He's come to the house a couple of times. He lives just down the street from us."

"Where do you live?"

"Uptown a bit. Near Fern Drive."

"Fern Drive," said Rick. "That's up near Acorn Place, isn't it?"

"Yes, that's right," said Curtis.

"Of course it is," muttered Rick, leaving Curtis completely flummoxed by the sudden shift in his tone. "Listen," said Rick. "I have to go. I'll see you tomorrow afternoon."

"Of course," said Curtis, and he watched Rick stroll over to Esther and speak urgently to her. She reached out as though to stop him, but he twisted away and stomped out the door.

Esther looked distraught for a moment before she quickly arranged her features into something professional and friendly when a new customer approached the counter.

What had he said to upset Rick so much? He needed to know, and he was going to wait until Esther had a minute to speak to him.

How could an attempted job offer end so badly? Esther looked distracted while she took the customer's order, and her eyes kept straying toward his. She handled the transaction well, but he could tell something was on her mind.

A few minutes later, she headed toward him. Maybe he would get an answer after all.

"Hi," she said, taking the seat that Rick had vacated a few minutes earlier. "Just want to apologize for Rick. He's a bit sensitive right now."

"He looked angry," he said. "I'm not sure what I said."

"I'm not sure either, except it seems to have something to do with our parents' house. What did you say to him exactly?"

"I just said that I think Anthony knows his son. They may even work together at Orca Sound. I'm pretty sure he's come to our place a few times. He only lives a few blocks away, near Acorn Place."

"Ah," said Esther. "Now I understand." She sighed. "Acorn Place is where our parents live, and I imagine Rick is now convinced that his son has been living there for the past few months, with our parents' knowledge. He's likely looking after the place while they're in Costa Rica for the winter."

"And he's mad because he didn't know?"

"He's mad because our parents never told him," said Esther. "Though I imagine Cameron asked them not to. And now…" She paused a moment, her elbows on the table. "Oh, no," she whispered. "This isn't going to go well."

"What's not going to go well?"

"If my brother charges up there, Cameron is either going to feel attacked, or betrayed by our parents, or both. I tried to stop Rick, but he's determined. I might as well try to stop a hurricane."

"I wish I'd known," said Curtis.

"I'm sorry I didn't tell you about Cameron. It's just that Rick's a private person, and he wouldn't have wanted me to say anything. Besides, I've already meddled enough."

"What do you mean?"

She bit her lower lip. "I went to the hotel to try and find out about the company he worked for. There's an employee there, Brooke, who used to work for me. You might remember her. She went to speak to him and left him a message that I had been there. I get the feeling they may be good friends."

"Maybe more than good friends. She's been to my place as well to watch a game with Ant and Cam."

"Right, so maybe she's his girlfriend. Oh, dear. I hope I haven't put her in an awkward position."

"Rick was bound to find out where he lives sooner or later," said Curtis. "Now, all we can do is wait and see what happens next."

"I suppose," said Esther. "I just hope Cameron is happy Rick made the effort to find him. Maybe it will all be okay." But the tension in her jaw indicated that she thought otherwise.

"You care a lot about him, don't you?"

"Yes. My brother has always been good to me. In fact, he saved my life." The unexpected confession hung in the air between them.

"Saved your life?" This was news to him—yet another example of how little he knew of her life. He had known Esther in high school, and he knew her now, but there was a gap of several years that he knew nothing about.

She looked up at him sharply, as though she wanted to take back what she'd just said. "It's a long story."

"I have time," he said, "if you want to share."

She gazed at him steadily as though weighing something in her mind. Her eyes softened for a moment, and he waited for her to let him in. Then the bell over the door rang, and she looked up abruptly at the customers coming into the bistro.

"Maybe one day," she said.

Curtis nodded, understanding that her story still held pain despite the years that had passed. He hoped one day she would share it with him. "Well, I'm always here to listen," he said, wishing he could pull her into his arms and reassure her. She looked sad. Or maybe regretful?

"I know, Curtis. You're a good friend."

Good friend. Was that what he was? He supposed they were good friends, and there was nothing wrong with good friends except… He looked at her more closely, and it dawned on him. He didn't want to be her friend.

He wanted more.

Much more.

But how could he ever tell her when she kept herself so closed off to him? When she never told him anything? It was a big barrier: although she saw him as a friend, she didn't completely trust him.

And he didn't know what more he could do to earn her trust.

"The room looks nice," she said, turning the conversation to a safe subject. "And it will be nice to get the boxes moved downstairs. Pearl seems to be enjoying having more places to hide, but I find them bothersome."

"So Pearl hides from Rick too?" For some reason that made him feel better. "I thought it was just me."

"No, she's a pretty equal-opportunity hider," said Esther. "I just happen to know the way to her heart."

"And what is that?"

"Salmon treats," she said. "That cat loves them more than catnip."

"Ah, I wondered if there was a secret."

"I suppose everyone has a secret something," said Esther.

"Yeah?" said Curtis. "And what is your secret, Esther?"

"Mine?" She laughed.

"Yes. What is it that you want above all else?"

"Never thought about it much," she said lightly. "I guess if I want something, I just go and get it—or make it—myself."

"Hmm," he said. "Is there anything that you can't do for yourself?" He looked at her steadily, and she blushed. He had struck a chord.

"Well, I suppose I appreciate people who are easy to get along with, and not having to struggle to find staff."

"I understand all the challenges of your professional life, but is there something missing in the rest of your life? Something personal you want or need?"

"Maybe," she said, just as the little bell over the door rang again. They looked up. "But right now I have to go." She stood up and pushed the chair back into place. "See you tomorrow?"

"Yes, of course," said Curtis, and as she walked away, he added, "Maybe by then you'll have an answer for me."

If she heard him, she didn't let on, just rushed toward the counter. But when she turned to face the growing line, he was pretty sure the pink tinge to her cheeks wasn't from exertion.

CHAPTER 10

Esther worked behind the counter until the initial rush was over and then slipped into the kitchen, away from the prying eyes of Curtis, who was still sitting where she left him. A dirty soup pot was sitting in the large sink—a job that required scrubbing and effort, and came with the bonus of letting off her frustration.

She grabbed her old apron from the hook and wrapped it around her waist, slipped on a pair of rubber gloves, picked up a scrub brush, and bent over the large pot. The kitchen's warm air hummed with the rhythmic clatter of dishes and the soft hiss of the coffee machine out front. Joel, the dishwasher, and Murial, the afternoon cook, stepped carefully around the kitchen and ignored her for the most part. Good. It gave her peace to think.

The conversation with Curtis had touched on things she needed to keep to herself. And his question about what was missing in her life? That had really discon-certed her because she knew exactly what was missing in her life—and she knew she couldn't have it.

Instead, she tried to focus on what she was grateful for. Her business was doing well, even better than it had before the pandemic. She had friends she saw often, hobbies she loved, and opportunities to work in her community and help others. She had family who loved her, and even her cantankerous, antisocial cat adored her.

But she was missing companionship.

She finished scrubbing and rinsed out the soap, bending to look at the pot again and make sure she had cleaned it before hoisting it out of the sink and putting it in the dishwasher to be sanitized. After turning on the machine, she peeled off the gloves and hung up her apron to dry.

Things weren't so bad. She had her independence. And though it would be nice to have someone to rely on… to have a partner…

A Curtis…

She could never tell him.

Not when he was still in love with his wife. So she would continue to keep him at arm's length, because letting him get closer would only end in pain and rejection.

She was about to peek and see if it was safe to return to the front when the back door to the kitchen whooshed opened and in stepped Rick, a scowl on his face and a thundercloud above his head.

"Hey, you're back," she said, instinctively trying to lighten the atmosphere. "Do you want a coffee or something?"

"No," he said. "Do you have a minute?"

"Sure," she said carefully.

He glanced at Joel and Murial. "Maybe we can go upstairs?"

"Of course." She walked toward him and said over her shoulder, "I'll be back in a bit."

"Take your time," said Murial.

As they walked around the building to the door to the apartments, Esther realized that it was not so much a thundercloud over Rick's head as just a deep sadness. She hoped there was something she could say or do to help relieve his pain.

When they got upstairs, he paced around her small sitting room, much smaller than normal because of the additional cardboard walls. She was glad the storage room would be done soon, though carting everything back downstairs was going to take a while.

"He didn't see me."

"I'm sorry," she said, putting her hand on his arm. "Do you want a hug?"

"What?" he said, looking down at her.

"You just look like you need a hug."

"We aren't a huggy family."

"I hugged you the other day, and it felt good. Maybe we should be more huggy."

He smiled, hugged her close for a long moment, and then stepped back. "Thanks. That did feel good."

She laughed. "Now that that's over, let's talk about what happened. And about what we might be able to do to make it better."

He paced again, and she let him. Her brother wasn't one to sit still, though she did find his restless energy a little distracting. So did Pearl, who was watching him from behind a nearby box. Her eyes followed his steps as though she were thinking of pouncing or, more likely, escaping if he pounced on her.

Pearl hadn't been treated well by her first owner, which the shelter guessed had been a man. She didn't get close to men.

Rick paced some more, then ran his hands through his hair and sat abruptly on the chair to face her. Pearl vanished.

"Start with the beginning. Where did you go when you left here?"

"I went to Mom's house."

"And?"

"And I watched him. He was out front, mowing the lawn. His girlfriend—I think it must be a girlfriend—was holding a bag for him while he put the grass clippings in. He looked happy."

"That's not bad, is it?"

"No. I just sat there in the car, feeling like a private investigator or peeping Tom or something, and I realized how far outside his life I am." He stood again and began to pace some more.

"So when you say he didn't see you, you mean he wasn't even aware you were there?"

"Huh?" He looked up at her and then ran his hand through his hair again. "I didn't get out of the car. He looked happy there without me."

"Well, some of that is kind of normal, isn't it?" she said carefully, not wanting to upset him. "Children grow up and move on with their own lives." She held her breath. She wasn't used to seeing Rick so vulnerable.

He looked down at her, his eyes filled with pain. "But don't they at least visit, or phone? I know his friends see their parents all the time."

"Maybe they live close by," said Esther. "You saw Sean pretty regularly when you lived in Nova Scotia, didn't you?"

"Yes, but he was running the business, and I was helping him get set up. He never moved away."

"Sometimes they have to move away," she said, shrugging nonchalantly. She forced herself not to point out that Rick had left home when he was younger than Cameron, and rarely visited. "And you must admit Vancouver Island is a very long way from Nova Scotia. He would have been closer if he'd moved to France from that end of the country."

"But why not call at least, so I knew he was okay?"

"That was down to Dana's interaction with him, wasn't it?"

"I suppose," he said. "But why did he feel he had to come out here to work in audio? There are companies out east as well."

"Maybe he got an opportunity here," said Esther.

"Do you know something more?" asked Rick. "If you knew, you would tell me."

Esther shook her head. "Nothing specific about his opportunities, but if what Curtis says is true, and he's working for the company that Anthony is working for, then maybe he's hoping for a break. The company gets subcontracted when the film industry needs locations. And we do have a lot of filming here."

"Right. I guess that makes sense." He sat again and seemed a bit calmer.

Esther focused on letting the tension in her neck dissipate. "If he could get cheap rent for a few months—and I can't imagine Mom and Dad charging much, if anything—then it makes sense that he might want to try his luck here for a bit. Vancouver is expensive."

"Why didn't Mom say something?" he asked.

"Maybe she thought you knew?" she ventured. As soon as she said it, she knew that wasn't true.

"They didn't even tell you he was here," said Rick, and she blushed, caught.

"I just realized that when I said it out loud. Maybe Cameron asked them not to say anything until he got work. I'm not sure." Though it made sense.

"But still…"

"Mom probably didn't want to be involved in anything between you and Cameron. She hates that you and Dad don't get along and probably figured you wouldn't be happy if he stayed here."

"Why would I not be happy that he was safe and had a roof over his head? It's been killing me to think of him living in a tent or a flophouse or something."

"Well, in her defense, she probably didn't know you were worried. It's not like you call home often." She admonished gently, though she wanted to whack him upside the head. It was hard to be patient with the dissonance between her father and her brother. She had forgiven their parents, and, in her opinion, she had more to forgive than Rick did. Or maybe not. She hadn't been close to her brother during his final year in high school; her friends and music had taken up much of her time. But, knowing their father, the pressure must have been considerable. After all, that same pressure had landed on her shoulders when he left home.

"I just wish things were better between us, like when Cam was younger. We had so many things we enjoyed doing together."

"Have patience. Maybe he'll come around."

"Why would he? He hasn't even stopped by to say hello or texted me back or anything."

"Well…" She paused.

"What? What do you know?" He sat again and looked straight into her eyes, searching for any hint of an answer. She was going to ease his mind.

She held up her hand to stop the questions. "I have something else to tell you, if you promise you won't act on it."

"What?" he asked, his jaw clenched. She waited patiently until he relented. "Okay, I won't do anything. So tell me. What?"

"I think I know his girlfriend." She told him of the encounter she'd had at the hotel.

"Do you think she would help me to talk to him?" he asked.

"Well, I hesitate to ask," said Esther. "I only suspect they are close. Nothing confirmed, really. It was just a vibe I picked up."

"A vibe?"

"A feeling," she said. "But I asked her to let him know I was asking about him. That I would love to see him. So *he* knows that *I* know he's there."

"And this encounter with the girlfriend was when?"

"This morning, when you were up at the Shack. She was at work. She really hasn't had time to talk to him about it yet."

"I suppose," said Rick.

"And he knows you're here, Rick. Just be patient."

"That's not something I am good at," he said.

"I realize that, but you will have to give him the space to return. Like you said yesterday, the ball is in his court."

"Unfortunately, the kid was never a great tennis player," mumbled Rick.

"Give it time," she said, smiling at his attempt at levity then glancing up at the clock on the nearby mantel. "Speaking of time, I have to go downstairs to make sure the staff have had their breaks."

"I'll come and help," said Rick, standing up and

pulling her into a hug. "Thanks for listening. I'm glad I have you to talk me off the ledge."

"Not a problem," she said. "Shall we?"

He walked ahead of her, and she glanced back to make sure the cat's water bowl was still full. Pearl's white paw was reaching out from under the couch. "I'll see you later," she said, bending down and looking at the cat.

Meow, said Pearl in response. Esther reached under to give Pearl a scritch behind the ears then left the apartment and locked it behind her.

When she got to the other end of the hallway, she found Rick chatting with her neighbor, Yvonne, who was carrying two paper bags of groceries and looked like she just wanted to get past him.

"You sure you don't need any help with those?" he asked. Yvonne shook her head, her sleek dark ponytail swishing against her shoulders. She eyed the stairs as though determining the safest route around him.

When she saw Esther, a spark of hope glinted in her eye. "Hello, Esther. How are you today?"

"Hi, Yvonne." Esther nodded toward Rick. "I see you've met my brother. Rick, this is Yvonne. She lives across the hall from me."

"Yes," said Yvonne, looking so uncomfortable Esther was sure she would break out into hives if they stood there any longer.

"I was just offering to assist," said Rick.

"I don't need any help," Yvonne said to Rick.

Esther rose her eyebrow at her. Yvonne really did sound cold sometimes. Yvonne must have noticed Esther's expression because her expression faltered. "Thank you. I'm sure you have other things to do."

"Okay," he said, stepping away so she could carry on up the stairs. "Though it's no trouble."

"I said I'm fine," she mumbled under her breath as she struggled up the next few steps without the use of the handrail.

"Well, maybe I'll see you around," said Rick to her retreating back. He moved out of Esther's way so his sister could go down the stairs ahead of him.

"Maybe," Yvonne said, without looking back.

Rick watched her a moment longer then reluctantly followed Esther. "What's with her?" he asked when they were out of earshot.

"She's a loner," said Esther, trying to keep her less-than-positive opinion of her meddlesome neighbor to herself.

"Well, she's a damned attractive loner," said Rick, taking a few more steps. It was then that they both heard a loud rip and a curse emitting from the lips of Rick's attractive loner. A moment later, a couple of oranges bounded down the steps toward them.

"Excuse me, Esther," said Rick, grinning. "I think I need to be neighborly after all."

"It's your life," said Esther. She picked up one of the oranges and handed it to him. "But I'm warning you, that one can be pretty cold."

"Thanks," he said, taking the orange from her and bending to pick up three others that had landed on the steps. "I know how to heat things up. I'm an electrician." He grinned, then took the steps two at a time to offer his assistance.

Esther shook her head. What was it about Rick's taste in women? Though if she had to choose between

Dana and Yvonne, she supposed Yvonne might be an improvement.

But she didn't have time to think about it. She had a business to run, so she walked back down to the restaurant and let herself into the kitchen, where she stopped to wash her hands.

At least Yvonne had given Rick something to focus on besides his problems with his son.

And for that Esther was grateful.

CHAPTER 11

The following afternoon, Curtis waited while Rick brought Esther to the storage room to look at the work they had just completed.

"Well, what do you think?" he asked when she arrived.

"You've done such a great job," said Esther. She looked first at Rick, then at the three students—who beamed—and finally at Curtis. "Thank you," she said, her eyes brimming with tears.

"Our pleasure," said Curtis.

"Okay, if you're good with this, we're going to get the boxes now," said Rick, beckoning the students to follow him.

"I'm glad you like it," said Curtis. "I wish you had said something weeks ago. I would have helped earlier."

"I thought that the insurance would fix it, but they wanted so much. And with the deductible… Well, it made more sense to do it myself."

"You've done so much to help me with the band, and the Men's Shack, and everything, I would have been happy to help."

"And you did," said Esther, smiling. "Thank you." She squeezed his arm. "I appreciate it. You just need to send me the bill for the supplies."

"It wasn't much," said Curtis. He didn't want to ask for money.

"Then the bill will be low," said Esther. "And I want the students to get a fair wage. Send me the bill, Curtis."

He nodded, though he wasn't pleased with the idea. He had wanted to do this for her. But in true Esther fashion, she would not let him help. He should have known better.

"I'm going to the kitchen to get some food for you folks. Do you think your crew might like flatbread this time? I have some fresh shrimp I can add to it."

"Sounds great," he said, "but give us about forty-five minutes. We've got some cleanup to do."

She scurried from the room, and he sighed and went in the direction of her apartment to help carry down some boxes. What did he need to do to get her to open up to him? To trust him? To see him as more than just a friend?

He flattened himself against the stairwell as the students came down, carrying a box each. "Do you know where they go?" he asked them.

"Rick told us."

"Good," he said, walking past them to the apartment.

"Hey," said Rick. "Can you wait here until I get back? I don't want to leave Esther's apartment open."

"This isn't a big city," said Rick.

"Still, I'd feel better if one of us was here to make sure the cat doesn't get out."

"Right, the elusive cat," said Curtis. "Have you met Pearl yet?"

"I startled her one day and saw her flash by," said Rick, "but otherwise, no."

"I've never met her either," said Curtis. "Though she did try to grab my foot once."

"Reaching out or attacking?"

"Attacking, I expect."

"Esther said the cat's a rescue that wasn't treated well."

"Maybe that's it," said Curtis.

"I'll be back in a bit," said Rick. "The others will be back soon. He pointed to the boxes. "These are all paper products and not very heavy. They go on the top shelves. Those"—he pointed to smaller boxes—"are heavier and should be on the bottom shelves."

"I'll let them know," said Curtis, stepping inside the apartment and closing the door, then opening it again to let the students in to grab another load.

When they were gone again, he went to the bedroom

where Rick was staying and shifted some of the boxes out to the hallway.

"Thanks for doing that," said Rick, as he poked his head into the apartment a few minutes later. "It will help us streamline this."

"Not a problem," said Curtis. And once Rick was gone again, he shifted the rest of the boxes from the room and, careful to watch for the cat, pushed them out the door to the hallway.

Finding no further boxes in Rick's room, he peeked into Esther's bedroom, breathing in the light scent of fresh linen. The room was decorated in greens and blues, and a stack of books sat on the bedside table. He wondered what she was reading but he didn't dare step further inside. There were no boxes in here.

As he eased the door closed again, he noticed a guitar on a stand in the corner. She'd never mentioned that she played guitar. Why wouldn't she have told him that? It was something he loved. What else didn't she share? He heard footsteps coming toward the apartment, so he quickly pulled the door shut and walked into the living room, eager to put distance between himself and her bedroom door. There he found several more boxes piled near the window. He was wiggling one toward the hall when Rick came in.

"We've just about got them all?" he asked.

"Only about six or seven more," said Curtis, waving his hand toward the living room.

"Great. I'll put this one out there for the crew."

"It's heavy," said Curtis, "and taller than the others."

Rick grabbed the other side of the box to help. "I see what you mean. I'll get a couple of them to help me with this one. Meanwhile, if you put the rest of these out in the hall, we should be finished in about fifteen minutes."

"Let them know there is a reward at the end," said Curtis. "Esther is making flatbread."

"I love her flatbread," said Rick. "Especially the shrimp and pesto."

"Esther is a great cook," said Curtis. "Why do you think I come for lunch so often?"

"Must be the cooking," Rick said, waggling his eyebrows at Curtis in a way that made heat rise up Curtis's neck to his cheeks.

"Esther makes everything taste great," said Curtis, turning toward the living room toward the boxes. He could swear Rick was laughing as he walked away down the hall. Was it that obvious that he was attracted to Esther? And if it was, did that mean she knew he liked her, but wasn't interested in him?

He worked steadily for the next few minutes, setting the boxes outside in the hall, and when he was done, he looked around at the dust. He wanted to sweep it up but wasn't sure which cupboard held the broom and dustpan. He had already intruded on her privacy by looking into her bedroom, so he sat down on a nearby sofa to wait, his back ramrod straight as though he were waiting in the principal's office at school. Why did he feel so awkward?

He heard the crew come back for another load. In the silence that followed, he looked around the room. He hadn't been in it often except to wait for her on their Tuesday movie nights. A bowl of lilacs on the small dining table had seen better days, and there were a few landscape paintings hung around the room. As he sat, he realized his muscles were beginning to soften. The tension at the back of his neck was receding. Esther had a way of making him feel at home, even without being here. She had a way of making him feel close to her, of making him want to be closer.

How was he going to convince her to take a chance on him?

More footsteps came to the hall and left again, and he closed his eyes a moment. Rick would be back soon. He should get up to go.

He opened his eyes and noticed Pearl peeking out from behind the leg of a nearby chair. Curtis stayed still and watched the cat to see if she would come closer.

She crept a few more steps, watching him closely, and he smiled. The cat was a real beauty. Thick white fur, bright blue eyes. He reached out, beckoning to her, and she took a few hesitant steps closer.

"Come on," he said softly. "Come say hello."

The cat's ears came forward, alert, and she took a few more steps. He leaned forward, stretching his hand toward the cat, and she came a little closer, no longer crouching, walking more confidently. She was nearly there. "Come on," he said, coaxing her a little more.

And then the steps in the hall grew louder, the door opened, and Rick came in. "We're all done. Ready?" Pearl froze a moment then streaked back to the comfortable area under the chair.

Curtis sighed his disappointment. "Ready."

"This place looks a lot larger without all the boxes," said Rick.

"I was planning to sweep but didn't want to poke around in the cupboards."

"Never mind that," said Rick. "I'll do it later. Right now, there's some hot food waiting downstairs."

Curtis followed Rick out of the room, turning a moment to look back at the chair. Pearl's paw was sneaking forward again, as though she were waving goodbye.

Or beckoning to him, asking him to come again.

Only time would tell.

CHAPTER 12

*E*sther and Rick fell into a rhythm over the next few days. They worked in the kitchen together, shared breakfast and conversation, and then Rick would walk down the street to the nearby gym to work out while Esther opened the restaurant.

After his workout and shower, Rick would return, see if she needed any help, and if not, he would go up to the Shack to learn how to turn wood. He enjoyed the practice, he told Esther, and she was pleased he had something to keep him occupied.

When the next Tuesday rolled around, he still hadn't seen Cameron, but he was feeling less anxious about it. Perhaps because he knew Cam was safe—or perhaps because of the neighbor.

Rick had discovered that Yvonne left for work at nine, and he had begun the habit of leaving the apartment when she did so he could "casually" bump into her and walk with her to her dental office.

"Could you be any more obvious?" Esther asked him one morning as he was helping her with the baking. "I hope you aren't bothering her."

"No crime in walking the same direction as another person, is there?" he asked innocently.

"It's called stalking if it bothers her."

"Has she said something?" Rick looked genuinely concerned. "I wouldn't want to make her feel uncomfortable."

"I haven't seen her since we talked on the stairs," said Esther. "Though I will see her at choir on Thursday. We're having one of our last concerts in two weeks."

"Where's the concert?" he asked. "I'll have to get a ticket."

"Since when are you interested in choral music?"

"Since my sister began singing in a choir," said Rick. "Your choir was responsible for my ability to play sports, you might remember."

"I forgot about that," said Esther. "It worked out, didn't it? You and Dad really bonded over soccer."

"We did—until we didn't," said Rick.

"Maybe you can rekindle that feeling when Mom and Dad get back," said Esther.

"When is that?"

"First week of June, I think."

"That's in just two weeks," said Rick, his voice tightening.

"Yes."

"I wonder what Cam will do when they get back." He was trying to sound casual, but Esther knew the question had been occupying him for days.

"Well, they have an extra room," said Esther, watching him carefully. "Or maybe he's looking for another place to stay."

"Just wish I knew." Rick turned away, unable to hide the flash of pain in his eyes.

"Want me to ask Mom next time they call?"

"No. Don't."

"Have you given any thought to Curtis's offer?

"Yes. I start tomorrow. I just need to get my clearance done so I can work with youth."

"Congratulations. What's the project?

"Two new benches for the waterfront and a free library box for the literacy program."

"Those sound like worthwhile projects."

"And it'll be good to be paid for a change. I'm also looking for a place so I can get out of your hair."

"You aren't in my hair. It's been great having you."

"I don't think Pearl would agree. Still haven't seen her."

"She takes a while to warm up to people."

"A bit like her owner."

"What's that supposed to mean?"

"Nothing." He shook his head. "Sorry I said anything." He looked up at the clock, which had drifted close to nine.

"Gotta go."

"No rest for stalkers," quipped Esther laughing. But she made a mental note to ask Yvonne if he was bothering her. She still hadn't quite forgiven Yvonne for how she had poked her nose into the music store business, but she didn't want the woman to be a victim of an overzealous man—even if that man was her quite wonderful brother.

As she heated the milk for a latte for one of the customers, she considered what else she could do to help Rick and Cameron get together. She had given it time, told Brooke to pass on a message, and found out that Cam was spending time with Curtis's son. What she needed was a way to move things along.

And one of the best things to bring people together was food.

She would invite them to dinner. All of them. If Curtis and Anthony came, it would give Rick and Cameron a buffer. She would ask Curtis what he thought and invite them all for Sunday dinner. Her little apartment would be full to the brim, but they would fit.

And they would have to interact with each other. The only one who could get away without talking in a space that small was Pearl—and even she might be convinced to make an appearance if Esther served salmon.

Later that evening, Esther and Rick were relaxing in her living room when Curtis arrived to take her to the movies.

"What's on tonight?" asked Rick, reaching into a bowl of chips and flipping the channel to a game show Esther loathed.

"A rom-com," said Curtis. "Your sister's choice this week," he added in his defense.

"For the first time since forever," laughed Esther. "You have no idea how many adventures and thrillers I've watched in the past few years." She made light of it, but the idea of going to a rom-com had surprised her. Curtis always found a reason not to see one, so she normally watched them on television with Pearl or went to the theater with girlfriends.

"Have fun," said Rick. He turned to the television. "Chickens," he said.

"Chickens?" mouthed Curtis to Esther.

"He's watching a game show," she said, pushing him down the hall. "Let's go."

As they walked toward the theater, she said, "I'm thinking of asking Cam and Brooke to dinner on Sunday. Do you think Ant and you could join us?"

"I could ask him."

"It wouldn't be until about six thirty. I'm thinking salmon or roast beef," she said casually.

"You had me at dinner," said Curtis. "You know I love your cooking."

"But do you think Ant would come? I know he doesn't really know me, but I thought since he knows Cam, he could help smooth things over with Rick."

Curtis didn't answer. He just stepped in front of her to order the tickets.

"I mean, if you're busy or you think it would be too awkward, I understand. I'm just trying to figure out a way to get them to come together."

"I'll talk to Ant," said Curtis, holding the door for her. "Now, do you want popcorn or a candy bar?"

"I don't even know why you bother asking," said Esther.

"Popcorn it is," he said, stepping in front of her.

"I can get it," she said.

"I know, but it's my turn," he said, not budging.

"All right, then," she relented. "I'll buy next week."

He stepped forward, ordered, and waited a few minutes for their food to be prepared. "When was the last time Rick heard from Cam?"

"He hasn't contacted him for a long time. I'm worried. Just thought maybe I could nudge things along."

"I hope it works. Though I must admit I did my own nudging the other day. Sort of."

Curtis thanked the teenager at the concession booth, handed Esther a bag of popcorn with extra butter and a sparkling water, then picked up his own popcorn and cola.

As they settled into the reclining seats the theater had finally installed the year prior, Esther said, "Tell me about this nudging."

"Well, I asked Ant how well he knew Cam. He was reluctant to talk at first, but when I told him Cam was your nephew, he opened up a bit. He likes you," he said, looking at her.

"Well, I like Ant too," said Esther.

"No, I mean he really appreciates what you did for his mother and for us when she was so sick. It made him feel… What was the word he used?" He took a bite of popcorn and chewed a moment. "He said he felt like someone was watching over us. All the food you organized after Maggie passed, the extra help when we decided to put on the fundraisers. And you never told me you helped Ant get his job with Orca Sound."

"I don't think I was much help. Ant was looking for a job, and Ted was looking for help. All I did was introduce them. Ant did all the work."

"But it allowed him to stay in town. And, to be honest, Esther, I'm not sure what I would have done if both the boys had left home."

"Logan didn't leave home. He went to school. He comes home at least once a month."

"I know, but I was so grateful when Ant got that job. It meant he could work here, and it gave me a reason to get up and out. It was touch and go for me for a while, you know."

"I know," said Esther, patting him on the hand. "But you're doing much better now."

"I am, but I owe so much to you," he said.

"What are friends for?" she said, then pointed to the screen. "Now shush. The movie's starting."

She settled back into the seat, grateful that the theater was dark and Curtis couldn't see her face. Couldn't see the longing in her eyes. She wanted so much for him to care about *her*.

It was nice that he appreciated her actions, but it would be much nicer if he could appreciate her for herself. Sighing inwardly, she turned her attention to the movie, pleased that the actors were skilled enough to take her away from herself for a while. Soon she and Curtis were laughing together, and his laugh was the best sound she had heard all day.

Two hours later, they walked in silence down the darkened street toward her apartment. The familiar storefronts of Sunshine Bay were shuttered for the night, their windows dimly lit from within and casting shadows on the various window displays. They had made this walk many times before, passing the same brick and wood frames, but today the air felt charged, electric, and Esther couldn't put her finger on why.

"That was a fun film," she said, trying to inject some normalcy into the space between them.

Curtis glanced down at her, smiling softly. "A bit predictable but, yes, I enjoyed it."

"Rom-coms are supposed to be a little predictable," said Esther. "Like comfort food or a pair of old slippers. You get what you expect for the most part."

"Well, that's what I meant," he said. "It is a comfort to know how things will end up. Especially since so much in the world is unpredictable."

She didn't reply, just walked in silence, feeling as though a proverbial elephant was walking along the street with them.

Or maybe it was just a tiny mouse.

Either way, something was niggling at her.

Curtis was the first to interrupt the silence. "Esther?" He slowed his steps and turned to look at her, his eyes bright in the light of an overhead streetlamp.

She stopped only inches away. "Yes?"

He shoved his hands in his pocket as though girding his loins for something. If she hadn't been so curious, she would have poked fun at him for that. But she sensed that her usual attempt at levity would not be welcome tonight. What was this about?

Curtis took his hands out of his pocket and rubbed them on his slacks. Why was he so nervous?

"What is it?" Esther finally asked. "You look like you have something to say."

"Yes, I do."

"Okay, then, go on. I'm listening."

"Um." He rubbed his hands together. Was he cold?

She forced herself to be patient. But he really needed to hurry up. There was a cold breeze picking up, and she had only worn a light spring jacket.

"Esther," he began again, "I was thinking. While we were watching that love story today. Well, do you know that two years ago I couldn't have done it? Maybe even a year ago. Watching couples in love after Maggie died was just too hard."

"I'm sorry. I should have suggested another thriller," said Esther.

"No, that's not what I meant," he said, shaking his head and placing his hands on her shoulders—warm hands that warded away the cold. The feeling came as a shock at first. He had never touched her like this before.

She looked up at him and, as though just noticing his hands, he dropped them and shoved them back into his pocket, leaving her confused.

Her eyebrows drew together in concentration, and she forced herself to hold his gaze. To not look away. But it was hard. He had never looked at her this way before—with a touch of longing and regret. Her heart pounded hard, and she strained to hear what he was saying.

"What I mean is, things are different now," he said in low tones. "I don't feel that same ache when I think of Maggie's absence. And I don't feel the same survivor guilt I once did. Because that was a lot of how I felt. How could she—a wonderful mother, an excellent doctor and wife—die, while I lived?"

"I know," said Esther. "I know it's been hard."

"But in recent months things have shifted. I don't feel

like I'm betraying her by living anymore. It's okay to be happy."

"I see," said Esther, glad that he was having a breakthrough.

"No, I don't think you do see," said Curtis blowing out a breath. "Let me try this again." He looked up at the star-filled sky and then back down at her.

"Did you know that Tuesday evenings are my favorite time of the week?"

"I enjoy the movies too. It's great entertainment," she said lightly. He was suddenly too serious, and it was making her uneasy.

"Yes, the movies are fun to watch, but it's more than that, Esther."

"How?" she whispered.

"I look forward to driving over here. To hearing your comments about the trailers. To ordering one plain popcorn and one with extra butter. To running into people we know and having them wonder about…"

"About?"

"No," he said pulling his hands out of his pockets and placing them on her shoulders again. "Let me get this out."

"Okay," said Esther, blinking.

"What I am trying to say is that I don't know what this is between us, but…" He took a deep breath.

"Don't say anything we'll regret," she warned him, heart pounding.

"Esther, you and I have been friends for a long time."

"Yes."

"But in the last while, it's been more than that for me."

She wanted to jump up and down, reach up and pull him into her arms, hold him and not let him go, but instead she waited for him to continue.

"I have come to rely on you. No. It's more than that. I look forward to seeing you. To spending time with you for any reason at all."

"Tuesday evenings are my favorite night of the week too," said Esther quietly.

"Really?" He looked in her eyes. "Oh, Esther, I could just… just…"

"Kiss me?" she asked, smiling through misty eyes.

"Yes," he said, and the world seemed to pause as he pulled her to him. His lips found hers, tentative at first, then with growing certainty. Warmth blossomed between them as he deepened the kiss, and time dissolved until she became aware they were standing under the soft glow of a streetlight not far from her living room window. If Rick looked down right now… She abruptly stepped back, breaking them apart.

"Are you okay with this?" asked Curtis.

"Of course," she said, glancing up toward the window and realizing that right now she didn't care what Rick was doing. She grabbed Curtis's jacket and pulled him close again. "I just needed to catch my breath," she said, before picking up where they'd left off.

A long few moments later, they broke apart again, and Curtis smiled. They stood there holding hands and gazing into each other's eyes.

"Well, I guess that answers that question," he said.

"Which question?" she asked.

"Whether you feel this pull between us too. I've felt you pulling away from me lately."

"I've been worried about losing your friendship," she said softly.

"So have I." He chuckled.

"Where do we go from here?" she asked.

"Well, I guess we take it one day at a time. We don't have to rush anything. Just as long as we aren't standing still anymore."

"One day at a time is a good idea," she said, her old insecurities rising to the surface. "There are things you don't know about me, Curtis. Things that may make you change your mind."

"I can't think of anything that would make me change my mind," said Curtis, his eyes never leaving hers.

"I've chased men away before," Esther confessed, remembering the pattern of disappointment that had been her romantic life for decades. What if her need for independence and control eventually drove him away too? The mere thought of losing him made her heart pound louder.

"I'm not easily scared," said Curtis. "And you forget. You stuck with me through thick and thin these past years. You gave me the benefit of the doubt. I'm not afraid to do the same."

She looked up into his eyes and saw kindness and patience reflected back to her. "We can take it one day at a time," said Esther.

"Good," he said planting a quick kiss on her lips. "Now we should get home. We both have busy days tomorrow, and I have a new employee starting."

"Yes, Rick is excited," said Esther. "Thanks for doing that."

"I think I'll be getting the best of that bargain," said Curtis. "He is great with teens."

They turned toward her apartment building, her hand folded into his as though it belonged there. As though there was a chance this might just work.

When they got to the door, he said good night, but he didn't let go of her hand right away. "I'll see you tomorrow?"

"Yes," she said, looking down, feeling suddenly uncertain.

"I'll talk to Ant and see what he says about dinner," said Curtis.

"Yes, thank you," she said, continuing to look at her feet. What if this didn't work? She would miss him so much.

"Esther," he said softly, "look at me."

She looked up at him, and he smiled. "I meant what I said. I think we should take this slow. I just wanted to know if there was some hope that we could be more than friends."

"Right," she said, looking down again.

"I needed to know if you might have"—he put a finger under her chin and drew her gaze back to his—"feelings for me that might grow. Have I got it all wrong?" His smile faltered.

"No," Esther whispered. "I just need you to have patience."

"Patience. I have that in spades," said Curtis, smiling. He pulled her in to give her a warm embrace. An embrace she could very easily grow accustomed to.

"Good night," she said. "I'll see you tomorrow."

"I look forward to it," said Curtis, kissing her one more time before turning and walking down the street toward his car.

Esther watched him go, then let herself into the building and climbed the steps to her apartment, touching her fingers to her lips and smiling to herself.

Perhaps companionship would be hers after all. She stopped before entering her apartment door and gave herself a hug, remembering how he had held her only moments earlier.

Companionship would be wonderful, but—and she could hardly believe she was daring to think it— maybe their friendship could bloom into what she really wanted, what she hadn't thought would ever be hers after forty-eight years. Maybe with Curtis she really could have more than companionship or friendship.

Maybe she could have love.

CHAPTER 13

*R*ick shuffled into the living room, rubbing his eyes. Esther's soft humming filled the space, the tune unfamiliar but pleasant—one of her choir pieces, if he had to guess. She looked different today. The early morning sun streaming through the window seemed to soften her somehow. She looked happy. Less stressed than he'd seen her in recent days. He wondered what had shifted in the last twelve hours.

"Morning, sis," he said, picking up the sweatshirt he had left slung across the arm of the couch the night before. He tugged it on. "What time did you get in last night?"

Esther didn't even turn, just kept humming as she padded around the kitchenette. "Around nine thirty. You were snoring, so I didn't dare wake you. I know how crabby you get if you're up too soon."

He let out a short laugh. "Fair. Good movie?"

"Not bad." She walked over to Pearl's dish and scooped food into the bowl as she did every morning. There was no sign of the cat, of course. Pearl still had not ventured out when he was around.

He watched Esther from across the room. Yes, there was definitely a spring in her step this morning.

"You seem in a good mood today," he said, trying to sound casual as he leaned against the doorway.

"It's Wednesday. I have a meeting with the downtown businesses." She walked up to him and gave him a pat on the arm. "Ready?"

"Is that all?" he asked, following her down the hall.

She paused when she got to the top of the steps and turned to him. "Well, if you must know, I am working on a bit of a surprise."

That caught his attention. "A surprise for me?"

"I'll let you know more when I know," she said, her eyes dancing with mischief as she pushed open the back door and they walked around to the bistro. She unlocked the door. "Almost ready for breakfast?"

He gave a nod. "Yeah. I'm starving."

"Me too," she said, taking an apron off the hook near the door and putting it on. "What should we have?"

"Why don't you get started on the croissants and muffins, and I'll make the omelettes?"

"I was hoping you'd say that."

"I know. I can read your mind."

She laughed and walked toward the freezer to pull the croissant dough she had left there the night before. He beat the eggs, grated some potatoes for shredded hashbrowns, and put bread into the toaster. He liked his mornings with Esther: working side by side, sipping fresh hot coffee, and eating breakfast while they waited for the pastries and muffins to bake.

He wasn't sure how long he'd stay in town, or what would come next with Cameron or even with his father, but this… This felt like something solid, and he was surprised how quickly he had adapted to this new routine.

Rick lingered in the kitchen long after the baking was done and Murial had arrived to cook the breakfast orders. He sipped a second cup of coffee while Esther went out the front to let in the staff and early customers. She hadn't elaborated on that "surprise" comment, and it was hard for him to forget. What was she up to?

He ruminated a bit longer but decided it was probably something minor. He had to get going. It was nearly eight and he hadn't left for the gym yet. His whole routine—though only a few days old—was off this morning.

Normally he would be halfway through his gym routine by now so he could be home by eight thirty, showered, and ready to accidentally bump into Yvonne before starting the rest of the day. He thought about her. Did she mind that he walked alongside her most days to the dental office? Maybe she was merely tolerating him or, worse, feeling like he was stalking her but too polite to say anything.

They had had some nice conversations, though— hadn't they? He thought about their morning ritual and realized they didn't really talk much. Yvonne wasn't exactly a ray of sunshine in the morning—or ever, come to think of it—but there was something grounding about walking beside someone who didn't feel the need to fill the air with words.

At least he found it grounding. Maybe she just thought he was a pest. They talked about little things —the weather, or the project he was working on—but for her part, she mostly just listened.

If fact, the more he thought about it, the more he realized that all he really knew about her was that she was a dentist, that she had lived in Sunshine Bay for several years, and that she was part of the choir—all information he had heard first from Esther.

Maybe his sister was right. He was stalking the poor woman. Well, today he would refrain. Instead, he went to the front of the bistro, where he was determined to lend a hand until nine fifteen, when he was sure she would have passed by and be safely in her clinic. Then he would go to the gym or, better yet, take a jog down to the waterfront before heading back to get ready for his first day at work, which would start at noon.

He pushed open the swinging door to the bistro and walked in behind the counter. "Need any help?" he asked Esther, who stopped mid-step and nearly crashed into him.

"No," she said. "Jessica and Nova and I have it covered."

"Oh," he said, disappointed.

"I thought you would be at the gym by now," said Esther as she began to make a coffee drink. "What's up?"

"Nothing," he said. "I… Nothing. I'm going for a run and then to work. I won't be home until after eight." He flattened himself against the back wall behind the counter as Jessica stepped past him to grab an order from the window.

"Okay," said Esther, flashing him a bright smile. "Have fun at your first day."

"Thanks," he said, scuttling out from behind the counter and giving her a little wave.

The bell above the front door jingled.

"Hey." Esther called him back. "Looks like we have a new customer." She nodded to the space behind him.

He turned and saw Yvonne enter the bistro, her hair in a halo of sunlight as she walked toward the counter.

"Good morning," he said as she approached, his stomach suddenly filled with butterflies. She was definitely the most attractive dentist he had ever met, but it was more than that. There was something compelling about her. Was it the way she moved with quiet confidence, or was it her cool indifference?

"Morning," she said evenly. To Esther, she said, "Could I have a medium roast, please? To go?" She handed Esther a traveling cup.

"Sure," said Esther, a smile creeping to her lips as she glanced at Rick.

"I didn't know you drank coffee," he said to Yvonne, who was now standing only a few inches from him.

"I usually have it before I leave home," she said, pulling a handful of change from her pocket and handing it to Esther.

"And today?" asked Rick.

"Today I realized I was out of coffee," she said. "So here I am. Esther's coffee is always good."

"So, you're on your way to the clinic?" he asked unnecessarily. "Do you mind if I tag along? I was going to go for a run near there." Though the waterfront where he had planned to run was in the opposite direction from Yvonne's clinic.

"It's a free country," she said. "Thanks, Esther."

Esther nodded, her eyes dancing as though she were going to burst into laughter any minute.

"Shall we?" he said, sweeping his arm ahead and urging Yvonne to leave before Esther lost control of her mirth.

"I didn't expect to find you here. Thought you would be at work by now," she said when they fell into step on the sidewalk.

"I got caught up here a little longer than normal. Esther has sprung a mystery on me." Why was he sharing this with her? He barely knew her, and he got the feeling that his sister wouldn't want a lot shared with Yvonne. There was a coolness between them that he would need to ask Esther about. Soon.

Yvonne raised a brow. "Mystery?"

He shrugged. "Said she had a surprise for me. Refused to elaborate. And she's been looking a little smug."

Yvonne looked at him for a long beat, then let out a soft laugh. "It isn't being smug. It's…"

"What?"

"Esther is a maven." There was a hint of admiration in her voice. "She has a gift of connecting people and possibilities."

"She does?" Rick frowned, trying to reconcile this with the person he thought he knew.

"Yes. I've known her for a long time. Not well, but I have witnessed her in action. She has this uncanny knack for discovering exactly what someone needs— often before they know it themselves—and then finding exactly the right person to help them get it." Yvonne's eyes held a curious intensity. "It's almost like she sees threads connecting everyone, threads the rest of us are blind to."

"My sister does that?"

"Oh, absolutely," said Yvonne. "And it's obscure things, like matching a job seeker with an employer.

In my case, I was looking for a van recently and telling a mutual friend about it at choir practice. She must have overheard—"

"You mean she listened in?" The thought made him uncomfortable.

"Well, no, she's not nosy or gossipy like some people are. She just always seems to be around to hear things. Anyway, she mentioned to our mutual friend that she knew a person who was getting out of the food truck business and wondered if that might work for my purposes."

"What do you need with an old food truck?" asked Rick.

"Oh, I need it for my business," she said. "I'm going to look at the truck later this week to see if it will work."

"For your business?"

"I don't really want to say anything more until I figure it all out," said Yvonne. "I still have to look into permits to see if my idea is even viable. But I like the idea of using an old food truck. And, if it works, it will be because of Esther's imagination. Haven't you ever noticed that about her?"

"Not really," said Rick, considering what she was saying. "But I haven't seen much of Esther in a few years."

"Her wheels seem to turn in her head, and she gets that glint in her eye—like she's set a table for two and already decided what you'd like to eat, and you didn't even know you were hungry yet."

Yvonne came to a stop, and Rick realized they were in front of her clinic now.

She unlocked the door and turned toward him. "A lot of people in town have Esther to thank for bringing them together. She's like a matchmaker on steroids, and she does it effortlessly. It's her way of caring."

"I didn't know she did that." It was all he could think to say.

"Well, I'm running a little behind today, so I should get going. Have a good run," she said as she pushed open the door and stepped inside.

Rick stared at the door for a moment, then back at the empty spot where she'd stood. Two women in one morning, leaving him with more questions than answers.

"Great," he muttered to himself as he turned toward the waterfront. "Just what I needed."

*E*sther hummed the piece the choir would be performing the following weekend and moved around her little kitchen, ignoring the noise Rick was making in the bathroom down the hall.

She looked in the oven to check the salmon Wellington and then checked to see that the rice pilaf and vegetables were done. The dessert—an array of goodies she had made in the restaurant that day that included brownies and apple tarts—sat on the counter. Ice cream rested in the freezer.

There was a knock on the front door, and she glanced at the clock. Quarter to six.

She walked down the hall and knocked on Rick's door as she passed. "They're here."

"Coming," he said. They were the first words he had said to her in the last four hours. Nerves, she told herself. He had been hopeful when she told him Cameron had accepted the invitation, but in the hours since he had helped her with the baking that morning, he had retreated from the bistro, and she hadn't seen him since.

She pulled the door open to greet Curtis and Anthony.

"Well, hello."

"Yvonne let us in. She was on her way out to her mom's place," said Curtis, bending forward to kiss her cheek, a move that still took her by surprise.

"Brought you some flowers," he said, handing her a bouquet.

"And wine," said Anthony, proffering a bottle of white.

"Thank you both. Come in," she said, stepping aside. She led them down the hall and into the kitchen. "Rick is around here somewhere."

As if on cue, he entered the room.

"Hi," he said, taking their coats while Esther got their drink requests and a vase for the flowers.

"It smells incredible," said Curtis, taking a glass of iced tea from her.

"It's salmon Wellington," she said. "You do like salmon, I hope?" she said to Anthony.

"Looking forward to it," said Anthony taking a beer from her and going over to sit with Rick.

"They should be here soon," said Esther, walking over to the stove to ensure the food was still okay. "We'll eat when they get here, and then I thought we could play some cards or a board game or something."

"Sounds good," said Curtis, walking a few steps closer to her. "Don't worry, I'm sure it will all be fine."

She stepped back from the oven and looked up into his reassuring eyes. "I hope you're right. I didn't know what to do. I could have waited until Mom got back, but then Rick would be dealing with our father and Cameron all at once."

She looked over at her brother, who had pulled a deck of cards out of a nearby drawer and struck up a game of rummy with Anthony. "He's nervous," she said softly.

"Have faith," he said. "They'll be here soon."

Then the buzzer sounded, and she went to the intercom at the end of the hall to buzz them up. She waited, shifting from one foot to the other, until she could hear footfalls coming down the hallway. As they approached, she opened the door and smiled widely.

"Brooke, it's good to see you again." She gave Brooke a small hug and then stood back so she could get a better look at her nephew. "Cameron, I am so sorry I didn't recognize you when I saw you the other day. I had no idea you were in town, nor that you were six inches taller than me now."

"It's okay," said Cameron. "I should have probably told you, but…"

"It was complicated?" suggested Esther.

"Yes. I guess so." He smiled at her then, a genuine smile like when he was younger. Before the estrangement had begun in the family. And her heart lifted a little. Maybe this wasn't one of her worst ideas after all.

"Come in," she said, stepping back.

"Thank you," said Cameron, allowing Brooke to go ahead first.

"Oh, we brought you this," said Brooke, handing Esther a box of chocolate-covered ginger.

"My favorite," said Esther. "What a great treat."

"They're my mom's favorite too. That's why I remembered. No one else I have ever met likes them that well."

"Come in. I thought we would eat first and then maybe play some cards or a game. I wake up at five, so dinner is usually early."

"Sounds great, Esther," said Brooke brightly. "I've been waiting for this all day and didn't have a big lunch."

"If you give me your coat, I'll put them in Rick's room. Pearl is in my room for the evening."

"Pearl?"

"My cat. She isn't particularly social." She had left Pearl sitting on the windowsill, her tail twitching as though she knew company was coming. It was better she was out of the way for the evening.

As Esther took their coats and escorted them into the living–dining area, Esther briefly wished she could hide in the room too until the evening was over. Hopefully Curtis was right, and this would go well.

"Would you like something to drink?" Esther asked them. Rick rose and walked over to greet them.

"Rick, this is Brooke."

"Hello," said Brooke, looking up at Rick as though afraid he would growl.

Rick's face broke into a grin. "Nice to meet you," he said, taking her hand to shake. "Esther has told me great things about you." She returned his smile, and Esther felt a little of her anxiety melt away.

"Hi, Dad," said Cameron stepping further into the room.

"Cam," said Rick. "How are you doing, son?"

"Could be worse," said Cameron, giving him a lopsided smile.

"It's good to see you. Your hair's grown. Looks good."

A flash of surprise flashed across Cameron's face. "I was pretty sure you'd hate it," he confessed.

Rick smiled as though amused. "It suits you," he said. "Now." He rubbed his hands together. "Can we get you something to drink? A beer, iced tea, soda, wine?"

"I'm driving, so I'll just have a soda," said Brooke.

"A beer," said Cameron.

"Great. And I think dinner is about ready. Esther explained how she likes to eat early?"

"Yes," said Brooke, following Rick to the counter. He was pulling drinks from the fridge.

Esther relaxed a little more as Rick finished serving the drinks, directed everyone to sit down, then helped her serve the food.

"This looks great," said Brooke as she gazed at the dishes in front of her. "How did you get time to do all this?"

"I have a whole kitchen downstairs at my disposal," said Esther. "One of the many benefits of owning a bistro."

They settled around the table. Conversation started slowly—weather, the bakery, Brooke's new job at the hotel. Anthony was mostly silent, sipping his beer and eating his food as others talked.

Cameron, who had started out friendly, seemed to retreat into himself again.

After several moments of nothing but the scraping of knives and forks on china, Rick said, "Cam, I heard you and Anthony are working together?"

Cameron shrugged. "Yeah, it's been good."

Rick nodded. "Well, I'm glad you're doing something you like. Audio work… I never really understood it, but—"

"You never asked me to explain much either. I'm not like Sean," Cameron said, his voice low.

A heavy pause fell over the table. Esther froze mid-cut, her knife in her hand. Brooke touched Cameron's arm, but he didn't look at her.

Curtis cleared his throat. "You know," he said carefully, "I'd like to know more about sound engineering if you'd like to share. Or I can share what I've learned recently about writing funding proposals. It's really very interesting stuff."

"Please spare us," Anthony said, chuckling.

Esther exhaled and gave Curtis a grateful glance.

"Tell them about our latest contract, Cam," said Anthony. "We're going to be working with Back and Away media. On a feature film."

Cam smiled and began to tell them about what they were doing and where the filming would take place. "It's eight months' work," he said. "Now I just need to find a place to live."

"What are you looking for?" asked Rick.

"A room in a house or a bachelor place. I want to find something soon. Grandma and Grandpa are back in two weeks."

"Right," said Rick. "I had forgotten they were returning so soon." Though Esther knew darned well he hadn't forgotten. Why was he saying that?

"You and Grandpa still not speaking?" asked Cameron, taking a bite of food.

Rick sighed. "We don't do well in the same room."

"Seems to run in the family," Cam muttered.

Rick flinched. "Cam—"

"I'm not trying to fight," Cameron said, softer this time. "I'm just saying… maybe you and I and Grandpa… Maybe we suck at this."

Rick stared at him for a long moment, then nodded. "Yeah. I think maybe we do."

"Or maybe you used to," said Esther. "People can change if they want to. Now about that place to stay." Cam turned to look at her. "Do you want me to keep an eye out for you?"

Rick glanced her way with a strange look on his face. "You know people with places to rent?" he asked.

"I know a lot of things, big brother," she said with an impish grin. "Some of them are even useful."

They all laughed, and the mood lightened just enough for dessert.

It wasn't until plates were pushed aside and the coffee was brewing that Anthony broke the silence again. "So you two…" he said, looking from Esther to Curtis. "Seem to be spending a lot of time together. Do you have a new project?"

Esther opened her mouth, but Curtis spoke first. "Well, it's new. Though it's not a project this time, exactly. We decided this week to… well… we're dating," he said simply. "But we're taking it slow."

Anthony blinked. "Okay."

Just that. No smile. No scowl. Just… okay. But the quiet tension that followed told Esther it wasn't quite *okay*.

"Why have you never said anything?" Rick asked her.

"It's like Curtis said. It's new. We're just trying it on. Seeing if it works."

"Well, I, for one, am glad. You two have a lot in common."

"Early days," said Esther again, looking over at Curtis and Anthony. She hadn't thought that Ant would be opposed to them dating. She was sure that he liked her. But she should have anticipated it. She knew firsthand about tension between young men and their fathers. She had thought it was just in her family, but she was apparently wrong about that. It made her uneasy. The last thing she wanted was to be responsible for Curtis having strained relationships with his boys. Or, worse, estrangement, like her brother had from Cam and their own father.

"Who wants a game of crib?" asked Rick.

She looked up at him and smiled her thanks. He sent her a small wink in return. When in doubt, action broke up tension. Cards was a safe idea.

"Sure," said Anthony. "Come on, Cam. We'll take on you and Brooke."

"Okay," said Cam. He and Brooke shifted to the other end of the table.

"I'll help with the dishes," said Curtis, picking up two of the serving plates from the table and bringing them over to the sink. Esther loaded the dishwasher and put away the extra food in a container for Cam to take home.

"That wasn't a disaster," he said quietly.

"No," she agreed. "Not a disaster at all, but…"

"But?"

She lowered her voice so they couldn't be overheard by the others. "Anthony seems upset that we are dating."

"He'll come around. I'll talk to him. Should have talked to him already. It's just that this is so…"

"New?"

"Strange to think of it that way," he said, and she laughed.

"Curtis." Her voice caught, but she plowed forward. "I need to tell you something. But not tonight."

He touched her cheek. "Whenever you're ready, I'll be here."

And though it had been a long time since she had believed in a man she was romantically involved with…

She believed in him.

CHAPTER 15

On Tuesday evening, Rick stood on the edge of the community soccer field and eyed the gathering clouds that threatened to interrupt the game happening in front of him. Though it was nearly June, the weather had decided to be unseasonable again. A cool wind was blowing, and he hoped the second half of the game would be done before the rain started. He hadn't brought an umbrella, just a spring jacket that flapped slightly in the breeze. He pulled his collar closer around his neck and turned his attention back to the game.

Cameron had begun playing with a local beer league a month earlier and had arranged to go out for dinner with Rick after the game. He spotted his son near midfield, running toward the ball and then passing it to a teammate before running further down the field. Even from a distance, Cameron looked focused and confident, and Rick was proud to see him that way. Of his two sons, Cameron had been the less self-assured. Sean, on the other hand, was an old soul.

The whistle blew, and the game ended in a 2–1 win. Rick clapped along with the few spectators and waited for Cameron. His son was talking to one of his teammates, then he picked up his equipment bag from the sideline and walked toward Rick.

"Hi, Dad," he said, sounding a little guarded, "Thanks for meeting me here." He opened his bag and quickly pulled on a pair of sweatpants and runners. His cleats landed on the ground with a soft clunk, their soles streaked with mud.

"You played well," said Rick. "That assist? Beautiful."

Cameron gave him a small smile. "Thanks."

"So where do you want to go? Got any recommendations?" Rick asked, waiting for Cam to pick up his bag and join him. They walked across the field to Esther's car and climbed in.

"There's a café not far from here. The Bee's Knees. They serve burgers and fish and chips, that kind of thing."

"Sounds good. I'll let you navigate."

The Bee's Knees was a low-key restaurant with wooden tables, soft lighting, and enough background noise to keep things from feeling too intense. The hum of conversation and clink of cutlery filled the air, mingling with the aroma of french fries and fried onions. They each had a beer and a burger. Cameron talked a bit about the team and his job. Rick listened. He didn't offer advice. Didn't interrupt. Just… listened.

When there was a lull, Rick cleared his throat. "I wanted to say I'm sorry, Cam."

Cameron glanced up. "Huh?"

"For not being there when you needed me."

Cameron's jaw worked as he considered his reply. "I was mad when Mom told me you couldn't help. That I had to figure it out."

"I didn't know about that," Rick said. "But I should have."

A long pause stretched between them.

"I was talking to Brooke about it the other day. She said that maybe it was a good thing. That it forced me to find another way."

Rick forced himself to listen without interruption. Just nodded, encouraging him to go on.

"I might not have come to visit Grandma and Grandpa otherwise. I stayed with them for about two weeks, waiting for my last paycheck from Vancouver. I didn't freeload or anything." He looked up at his father and then back down at his beer before he continued. "I helped do things like shovel snow, change lightbulbs, and I even gave Grandma a hand painting their living room. I must have done a good job because they asked me to house-sit while they were away. They trusted me to do that. It felt good to be trusted. And then I got a job because Grandpa knew Anthony. So I guess maybe Mom was right? Or at least not as wrong as I thought."

"Why didn't you call me?"

"Mom told me not to call until I was on my feet."

"Is that why you asked your grandparents not to tell me or Esther you were here?"

"Mom said I should be doing it on my own," he said. "And I wasn't. I was relying on Grandma and Grandpa for a roof over my head."

"That's nonsense," said Rick. "No one gets started on their own. Not me, not even your mother."

"What do you mean?" asked Cameron.

"Your mother has a selective memory. When I left home, I had some savings, but only enough for some food and a ticket to Fort McMurray. I had a friend working there, and he gave me a couch to crash on. Put in a good word for me with the company. Helped me get my first job up there. No way could I have afforded it otherwise."

Cameron's mouth parted in surprise at this revelation, so Rick continued. "After I had been there for about six months, a journeyman took me under his wing and got me started as an electrician. He convinced me to go to school, get my tickets. If I hadn't had that encouragement, I doubt I would have done it. I had no confidence. Old Wilbur helped me more than he will ever know." He paused and thought of the older gentleman, and took a drink of beer in silent salute to his memory.

"So you think everyone has help?"

"Absolutely. People don't live in a vacuum, Cam. Your mother might think she did everything on her own. And don't get me wrong, she certainly made a success of her business." He looked up to make sure his son didn't think he was putting down his mother. "But she used our money to finish her education after you were born. And she borrowed money from the bank on the strength of her father's signature—he cosigned the loan. And I built the salon in a room off the back of the house—the one Sean moved into when he was a teenager. So, though your mother has done very well, and she's really grown her businesses, she did have help. She has forgotten that, I think."

"She never told me that. She said I needed to be stronger, like Sean. He's set up his business all on his own."

Rick sighed. "That's just not true."

"What do you mean?"

"Sean had help. I put the money into the business to start it up."

Cameron wrinkled his brow. "Yeah?"

"Sean is buying me out over time, but I helped him get a start using the proceeds of my business, just like I did with your mother."

"Oh."

"And I want to help you as well. I don't have a huge amount left, but I have some to help you with, and Sean will be paying me back over time."

"What about the sale of the house?"

"I left most of it to your mother. Things mean more to her than they do to me."

"So does that mean you're going to stay here for a while?"

"Yes. For a while. I signed a six-month contract with Curtis. Then I will either stay on, if they still need help, or find something else."

"Did Esther help you get that job?" asked Cam.

"She introduced me to Curtis, so I suppose so, yes," he said.

"Then I should probably take her up on her offer to help me find a place to live."

"I'm certainly going to. She knows practically everyone in town. In fact, Anthony said it was because of Esther that he got his job at Orca."

Cam laughed. "Are you telling me that, indirectly, my family helped me get my job?"

"I guess that's the case," said Rick. "Hadn't thought of it quite like that."

"Dad, are you sure you should be staying here? Sean must need help with the business."

"Sean is doing fine. More than fine. But I'll go back and visit him in a couple of months to see how he's doing. Meanwhile, I want to spend some time with you and Esther, and… I'm going to try with my dad. He's getting older, and if Esther can forgive him, I can at least try."

Cameron looked up from his beer again. "I've been thinking about the new place. Rent's not cheap, even here and… I don't know…" He paused as though trying to decide then gave a little shake of his head. "What do you think of getting a place together for a bit? It would save us both money."

Rick blinked. "You mean it?"

"We could get a place for a few months. Try it out. Not forever. Obviously. But… maybe we could do it for a while? Some of the locations for the film are down-island, so I'll be away quite often. And if you're traveling to Nova Scotia and such… we won't have time to get under each other's skin. Probably."

A slow grin spread across Rick's face. "You seriously want to live with your old man?"

Cameron gave a small smile. "Let's not make a big deal out of it. Just—maybe we can try reconnecting. Get to know each other better now that things are different. See if it works."

Rick raised his glass. "To new starts?"

Cameron clinked his beer bottle against Rick's. "New starts."

"I'll talk to Esther in the morning."

The next morning, Esther woke in a foul mood. Even Pearl, who usually snuggled for a bit, sensed her mood and kept her distance. Esther lay in bed, the evening before playing through her mind. She and Curtis had gone to the movies and watched another rom-com. He had even put his arm around her, made her feel close. But on the way home, he had pressed her.

"What did you want to tell me?" he'd asked.

"It will keep," she said, not wanting to ruin the evening.

"You know I'm here for you," he said.

And she wanted to tell him about her ex. How dangerous he was. How she had missed out on some of life's experiences because of how he'd treated her. How he had damaged her ability to trust men. Even her ability to judge character.

She didn't want to tell Curtis yet. She was enjoying this too much.

So she said no. And now he was upset, even though he'd said he had patience. She turned in her bed and beat at the pillow. It was all going to go badly again. He was bound to leave once he knew how stupid she had been. Her thoughts swirled like storm clouds, heavy and unrelenting. And what about his sons? If Ant wasn't happy with them dating, Logan might feel the same. He had been so close to his mother. She beat the pillow again and flopped over on her back, staring up at the ceiling.

She should never have let things go so far.

There was a knock on the door. "Hey, sis," said Rick. "You almost ready?"

"No," she said.

He paused. "You sick?"

"Nooo," she growled. She wasn't sick, and she had a bistro to run. She had to get up.

"Want me to get things started?" he asked.

Well, that was a good idea. "Yes!" she said loudly.

"Okay," he said. "See you in a bit."

"Thank you!" she yelled, but she was sure he was already out the door. Probably running away just like Pearl had.

Esther groaned again then dragged herself out of bed and into the shower, where she let the water beat against her skin. She scrubbed harder than usual, as though she could wash away the doubt that had settled in her chest.

By the time she made it to the bistro kitchen, Rick had already mixed two batches of muffins, put them in the oven, and started the coffeepot. The warm, yeasty scent of baking wrapped around her. She said thank you, then went to the corner of the kitchen and threw herself into baking and routine, kneading the dough with more force than usual, smashing her worries into the flour.

It didn't work.

Rick silently prepared their breakfast and placed it on the table, poured two mugs of coffee, and waited for her to join him. Esther sighed and wiped her hands on a towel before sitting down to enjoy the meal.

They ate in silence for a moment, until Rick leaned on the counter and broke the silence. "You look like you haven't slept."

"Maybe I haven't."

"You want to talk about it?" he asked.

"No." It came out sharper than she intended, but Rick didn't seem to notice. He just nodded and picked up his coffee.

"Okay, but while you're sitting here being miserable, I need a favor."

"What kind of favor?" she asked, hoping he wasn't expecting much today.

"Cam and I had a good long talk last night, and we've decided to find a place together."

"Really?" She was glad to hear they had come so far

in such a short time, and that Cam had responded to Rick's efforts to reconcile. "That's great news."

"Yes, we want to find something for a few months. Try it out and share the rent costs. You mentioned you might know someone who could help."

"Yes, I do." She smiled, relieved that what he needed would take almost no effort on her part at all. She really was tired. "I'll get you Sheila's number. She's a realtor, but she also has the finger on the pulse of the rental market. Just let her know I referred you. She'll know what's available."

"Thanks," said Rick. "I'll have to look for some furniture."

"Oh, I can help with that too. I know a woman who sells a lot of secondhand furniture for cheap if you don't want to pay full price right away. A lot of it is real wood that could be refurbished. You know, if someone had the skills and access to a shop where they could do that." She smiled.

"That would help too," said Rick. "Thank you. Now." He grew more serious. "About that thing that kept you up all night…"

She looked up at him, considering whether to tell him to leave her alone, but she decided to let him speak. He was persistent, and would only come back later to bother her about it again.

Seeing no resistance, he continued. "I know you are afraid to tell Curtis about your past, but don't you think he deserves to know what's on your mind? What your doubts are? He isn't anything like Seth— or any other guy you've met, I expect. He's a really nice guy."

She stared into her coffee, her fingers tightening around the mug until the warmth of the hot coffee seeped into her palms.

"Have some faith, and give him a chance to prove it," Rick said softly. "It's better than losing sleep over something that probably won't happen."

Esther let out a slow, shaky breath. He was right. It was time to stop hiding away secrets and pretending things hadn't happened.

"Okay," she said. "I'll talk to him."

Rick clapped a hand lightly on the table. "That's my sister."

She rolled her eyes but smiled. For the first time all morning, the tightness in her chest loosened a little.

Maybe Rick was right and, if she told Curtis about her past, it wouldn't be an end but a beginning.

CHAPTER 17

*R*ick and Curtis worked beside each other later that afternoon, cutting out the pieces for a bat box, the air thick with the scent of fresh-cut pine and sawdust. Though they were still waiting for the go-ahead for the project, they had decided to test the pattern, build a pup catcher and a box, and work out the kinks.

Once they had the pieces cut, they came together at a large work bench in the middle of the room, sat on stools, and assembled the pieces.

"Rick, can I ask you something?"

"Sure," said Rick, pulling out some small nails to hammer the pieces together. "What's on your mind?"

"Do you think Esther is over her husband?"

"She's definitely over him," Rick said, not looking up from the wood he was sanding. His voice was clipped.

"Are you sure? How long ago did he die?"

"What?" Rick stopped what he was doing and looked up at Curtis. "Seth's not dead."

"He isn't?"

"No. What made you think he was dead?"

"Something my wife said once," said Curtis.

"That's right, Maggie was a good friend of hers, wasn't she?"

Rick kept working, and Curtis stared down at the directions for the pup catchers without focusing on the words. "I once asked Maggie why Esther had never married, and she said that she had. That she was still getting over it.

"Then, after Maggie died, Esther seemed to really understand what I was going through. What grief felt like. So I assumed she had gone through losing a spouse like I had. To cancer or something. And that it must have been so devastating that she never spoke about him."

"No, Seth isn't dead," muttered Rick. "Though if he were, it would be no loss to the world."

"So he left her? What kind of a man would leave Esther?"

Rick tapped a nail into the wood, creating a ninety-degree angle, then picked it up to make sure it matched the picture they were following. "He didn't leave her. She left him."

"What?" Curtis looked over at Rick, and Rick lowered his eyes. "You need to talk to her," said Rick, picking up another piece of the box he was building and hammering in the nails.

Curtis's mind raced as he made sense of this new information. The man wasn't dead, and Esther had left him. Something must have been very wrong with their relationship for her to do that. And to never speak of it. Then he remembered something else she had once said.

"She told me you saved her life once. She wasn't speaking metaphorically, was she?"

The hammer in Rick's hand stilled. Then he set it down carefully. "No. But you really need to talk to her."

"What did he do to her?" demanded Curtis, anger bubbling.

Rick sighed heavily and looked up at the ceiling as though asking the rafters for inspiration. "Curtis, she is really private about this."

"Don't tell me her part, then. Just tell me a hypothetical story about what a brother did to save his sister's life."

"I can't," said Rick. "I'm sorry."

"I shouldn't be asking," Curtis admitted. "I just wish she trusted me enough to tell me. It seems to be a significant event that still impacts her."

"I understand. If it were me, I would want to know too. What I can say is that I have recently advised her, again, to tell you the story. So hopefully you will know more soon."

"Well, at least I know she isn't still pining after a dead man. I thought I was competing with a ghost."

"There are different types of ghosts, Curtis." Rick picked up the fourth wall of the house and paused a moment. "Out of curiosity, is Esther competing with a ghost?"

"No, at least not so far as I'm concerned. But my sons may take a little longer to accept her in this new role than I thought they would. Anthony's reaction surprised me."

"It'll take time," said Rick. "Listening to some of the men's stories in here has taught me that." Rick hammered on the roof and floor of the house and set it on the table in front of him. "There."

"Hey, that looks great."

"Putting together ten shouldn't take too long. We could have a bat box party."

"I expect to get the funding in the next week or so. Then we are ready to go."

They worked for another forty minutes, figuring out how the pup catcher went together and finishing off the box. By the time they locked up the Shack for the evening, Curtis was determined to make Esther speak to him. He always found it useful to talk about his loss, and he knew it helped the other men at the Shack. He was sure it would help her too.

CHAPTER 18

That evening, Esther waited on the corner for Curtis to park his car, her hands jammed deep into her jacket pockets. She shivered in the cool breeze and thought of what she had to do next.

She was determined to say something. She'd promised Rick. But as he approached, her heart started pounding, not with anticipation or joy at seeing him—though she did feel some of that. Unfortunately, tonight it was overshadowed by nausea.

What if he would regret getting involved with her? Or got angry? Or…?

She shook herself. Rick was right. Curtis deserved the truth — and a chance to walk away if he wanted.

He stopped in front of her and bent to kiss her cheek. "Well, where shall we walk to?"

"Down by the water?" she suggested, her heart hammering. "We can watch the sunset."

"Great idea," he said. "Then I can buy you a hot chocolate."

"Okay," she said, though she was doubtful he would stick around after he heard what she had to tell him.

They strode toward the bay. "Thanks for calling. I wasn't sure I would see you today."

Esther gave a small, wobbly smile. "I thought we should talk. I promised I would tell you something about my past. Something that seems to get in my way. And…"

He stopped and turned toward her, grasping her hand. "I'm listening," he said. "And I'm not going anywhere."

"Don't make promises you can't keep," she muttered, her voice barely above the crash of waves against the rocky shore.

"I don't," he said firmly. Now, shall we walk down to the shore before the sun disappears?"

Esther started slowly. "First, I owe you an apology. For last night."

Curtis looked down at her and shook his head. "You don't owe me anything, Esther. I just… I could tell something was bothering you, and I'm sorry I pushed so hard."

She nodded, swallowing hard. "It's hard for me. Trust, I mean. I've had people leave when they found out about my past. My first marriage—it wasn't good. And sometimes I still feel like… like it was my fault for not seeing it sooner."

She glanced up at Curtis, who was staring straight ahead, his face hard and his jaw tight. "You don't have to tell me everything today, or ever," he said. "But from what I know about you, I don't think you should take the blame if he…" He turned toward her then, "Did he hurt you?"

A tear slipped down her cheek before she could stop it. She wiped it away quickly.

"Yes," she whispered. "And I'm so embarrassed that I didn't leave sooner. I just thought that if I changed, if

I could anticipate his needs, if I was a better wife, then he would be happy."

There, she had said it. She held her breath and waited for his response.

"Do you mean to say he hit you?" They were nearly to the waterfront now, and Esther guided him toward a bench that overlooked the sea. There was no one nearby. She urged him to sit, and she joined him.

"Yes. But it didn't start out that way. It started out with just a harsh word, a correction. He was older than me, and I was only twenty when we married. Twenty when he convinced me to leave home for an adventure in the big city. I didn't really know any better. He was the first man who ever really paid me any attention. I thought it was true love. Ha." She scoffed at the naivete of her younger self.

"I could have done without that adventure," she continued. "Within three months, we had left Vancouver. Too expensive, he said, and I hadn't found work yet. So we relocated north to the small town where he was raised. Where his family was. His friends. The only friend I had was his sister-in-law. She would visit sometimes, introduce me to others, but Seth didn't really want me to get to know many people. He wanted me all to himself. It was romantic at first. But then it was lonely. I have never felt so lonely."

"Oh, Esther," he said, and she held up her hand.

"Let me get this out, please."

He nodded, and she continued.

"I was so far from home, and my parents told me when I got married that I had made my bed. We eloped, you see—I thought it was so romantic and would save Mom and Dad money. But they just saw it as a betrayal."

She looked out at the horizon, where the reds and pinks of the sunset were appearing. After looking in that direction for a few minutes, she turned back to him.

"I was there for four years. I called my parents on Christmas and birthdays, always perfunctory calls that Seth monitored closely. And Mom and Dad never called me, at least not that I was aware of. And they never visited. I learned later that they had tried to call, but that every time they did in Seth made an excuse. I was at work, or I was out with friends. The truth was that I was out working in the garden or helping on the family farm. Unpaid work, of course. I was lucky, he said, to get food and a roof over my head, because I was so bad at it.

Curtis nodded to show he was still listening, though she could see pain around his eyes at hearing these details.

"My parents were good parents, for the most part. I think I hurt them so much by leaving, and it was around that time that Mom's mother was suffering through cancer. Dad… Well, Dad just works harder when he's upset, which is what eventually led to his heart attack, I think."

"Parenting is hard," said Curtis. "You never really know if you're doing things right."

"That's the worst of it, I think. I always thought it would be nice to have children, but I don't think I'd have been the best parent. Not with how I felt about myself."

"So what happened? What made you finally leave?"

"He started to use his hands after our second year together. Before that he just told me how much of a failure I was and tried to give me advice about how to get better. I was on a constant roller coaster ride. Up for a couple of days, and then plunged down in the depths.

"Then, just after our second wedding anniversary, he slapped me. I don't even remember what I had done to deserve that, but I remember the slap. It made me smaller and smaller. More and more closed in. Whenever I had bruises, he told his family that I wasn't feeling well, and I saw fewer and fewer people. I didn't know what to do because he told me that if I said anything, he'd hurt me even more. Anyway." She took a long, settling breath and gathered herself together. Though it had been nearly twenty-five years since she'd left, the experience still had some power over her.

"One day he hit me really hard. We were out in the milking barn, and he lost it. He punched me, kicked me, and left me in a stall with one of the horses—I suppose so he could, if pressed, claim the horse had kicked me. Luckily my sister-in-law found me. Instead of taking me home, she took me to the hospital in the next town over, where I had surgery." She pointed to her cheek. And her collarbone. "He broke a few of my bones that time, and when the nurses asked who my next of kin was, she urged me to say it was Rick. Then she left the hospital and, to my knowledge, never told Seth where she took me. Rick was there when I got out of recovery. Two days later, he took me with him to his place in Kamloops. I lived with him for a couple of years. I got a job in the local bakery, saved up money for my training, and then when he got married, I went to school and eventually came back here."

"Wow," Curtis murmured. He moved his hand instinctively toward hers but paused, letting her choose. "I can't believe how courageous you were."

"It took me a long time to see it." Her voice cracked. "I thought I must be the stupidest person in the world to fall for that. To allow him to hit me. To believe that if I could just do things right, he would love me more, and it would all be romantic and wonderful like it had been the first few months. Of course, now I know that was a fantasy. And that I was better off alone."

"Is that what you still think? That you'd prefer to be alone?"

"Over that kind of relationship, of course. But if things were different, I think having someone to share my life with could be pretty wonderful. Pearl listens, and sometimes she even talks back, but her vocabulary is limited, and she doesn't know how to play crib or change a lightbulb."

He laughed. "Thank you for telling me. I know that was hard for you."

"It does get easier over time," she said, almost to herself.

"Now, come over here. Look at that color." He put his arm up on the back of the bench and urged her to snuggle into him. They sat there for another twenty minutes, watching the sun slip into the sea.

"Oh, I forgot to tell you," said Esther suddenly. "Cam and Rick are getting a place together. Sheila Sales already has a few to show them."

"And you will get your house back. I guess Pearl will be happy about that."

"She did come out and take a good look at him on Monday night," said Esther. "But as soon as he looked at her, she ducked back under the couch."

"Well, that's good news. Maybe Pearl will warm up to me too."

"Only time will tell," she said, leaning against his shoulder and sitting in the growing dark for a moment. For the first time in what felt like days, the tight band around her heart eased.

Maybe this was what hope felt like — fragile but worth holding onto.

Curtis stood up and held out his hand.

"Come on," he said. "Let's get that hot cocoa. You've had a rough day."

Esther hesitated for a second, but then she slipped her hand into his. His fingers closed around hers — steady, warm, no pressure. Just *there*.

Curtis led her down the sidewalk at an easy pace, not saying much. It was enough just to walk side by side.

After a while, he nodded toward the little chocolate shop near the bistro. "Here we go. They have great hot chocolate here. And I hear chocolate can solve most every problem." He held open the door for her, and she grinned.

"Is that a fact?"

"Absolutely. Ask anyone."

They ordered two hot chocolates — hers with extra

whipped cream, his with cinnamon sprinkled on top — and carried them outside.

"Do you want to come up?" she asked. "Rick's out tonight. He said something about watching a game with Cam."

"Sure." They walked up the stairs and went inside, where she put a few fresh-baked cookies on a plate to go with their chocolate. For a few minutes, they sat side by side on the couch and sipped their drinks in companionable silence. No expectations. No pressure. Just the two of them, a little battered maybe, but still willing to try.

Curtis set his cup down and turned slightly toward her. "I'm really glad you called, Esther."

She looked up at him, her heart fluttering in a way that wasn't fear this time — it was hope.

"Me too," she said softly.

Curtis brushed a stray lock off her forehead. "And I want to remind you, despite what you told me—or maybe because it showed me how strong you are— that I'm not going anywhere."

Esther didn't say anything. She just leaned her head against his shoulder and closed her eyes for a moment, letting herself believe it might really be true.

The weight of light paws startled her, and she looked down to find Pearl sitting on her lap, looking up at her.

"Oh, hello," she said.

Mroww.

"Curtis, this is Pearl. And Pearl, this is the man I'm dating, Curtis."

"The man you're dating, eh? I like the sound of that."

"You know, so do I," laughed Esther, surprising herself with how easy it was to slip into this new phase.

Curtis pulled her close and kissed her, and Esther laughed again — a real, easy laugh she hadn't heard from herself in a long time. Curtis joined in before pulling her close for another kiss.

Maybe, just maybe, she thought, she could trust this.

CHAPTER 19

Rick tightened the strap across the mattress in the back of Curtis's truck and gave it a final tug. "That's not going anywhere," he said with satisfaction.

Cam grinned from the curb. "You may have a future as a swamper if you want to give up woodwork."

Rick gave him a mock glare. "Watch out, or I'll start playing my country music full blast when your friends are visiting."

Cam shuddered. "You wouldn't dare."

They both laughed, easy and unforced. It still surprised Rick sometimes, how natural it felt spending time with his son again. The estrangement and awkwardness had fallen away because here they were, two grown men hauling secondhand furniture and splitting rent on a little two-bedroom bungalow with a crooked fence and an overgrown garden in the backyard. A garden he was looking forward to tackling with Cameron, planting something that could grow and thrive just like their rekindled relationship.

"You sure that will fit through the door?" Cam asked, eyeing the sofa that protruded out the end of the truck under the mattress.

Rick shrugged. "We'll make it fit. Or take the door off the hinges. I'm sure we can find a saw if all else fails."

"Ha! Funny guy," said Cam. "Let's get this home, and then we can pick up the bed frames and the table and chairs."

They climbed into the truck armed with Esther's list of addresses and contacts for furniture. So far, they had enough to get them through the first couple of weeks. They could add other items once they had more time.

Later, as they shoved the last of Cam's boxes inside, Rick swiped his sleeve against his brow. The rooms were still half-empty but could be filled over time. It was nothing a few rugs and additional pieces of furniture couldn't solve. Cameron came out of his new bedroom and smiled at his father.

"It's looking pretty good, Dad."

"We'll fix it up as we go," he said. "But it's a great start."

"Grandma and Grandpa will be home soon. Grandpa said he might have an extra coffee table in storage that we could have."

"We'll have to see what it's like," Rick said, not sure he wanted to take anything from his parents at this stage in his life. He hadn't had anything from them since he was eighteen.

"They were good to me, you know," said Cam, as though reading his father's mind. "When you… couldn't be."

Rick met his son's eyes and swallowed hard. "I know. And I'm grateful. They didn't have to take you in. But they did."

Cam gave a small, quiet shrug. "They didn't have to. But they *wanted* to. That makes a difference."

Rick sat on the arm of the couch, shoulders heavy. "I don't know what I'll say to my dad. We've always had a hard relationship."

"What happened?"

"I guess I'm still mad that they didn't help Esther when she needed it. And then, when I got married, they weren't very supportive. It's been messy for years, really."

"Then maybe it's time to clean it up."

Rick gave a humorless chuckle. "If only it were that easy."

Cam nudged his shoulder. "You and I are good now. The fact that you came all the way out here showed me that you weren't going anywhere. It meant something. Maybe Grandpa will feel the same?"

Rick let out a long breath. "One can only hope." He remembered a recent promise he had made to Esther, and how she had shown bravery by talking to Curtis. If his little sister could forgive after all she went through, then he could try to forgive too.

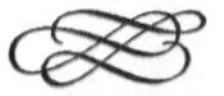

CHAPTER 20

Esther spotted them right away — her mother, Ruth, in her stylish cropped pants and blazer, and her father, Ian, looking fit and relaxed as he waited beside the luggage trolley.

She parked the car in the loading zone and ran to meet them.

"Welcome home! How was your flight?" She swept her mother into a quick hug then turned to do the same with her father, who patted her on the back. No, she reflected, they were not a huggy family, but her parents were getting better at it over the years.

"Good flight," said her father. "But long."

"I can imagine," said Esther, reaching for one of the suitcases. "Come, let's get you home. I've got the car right out front. And there's something special planned for tonight — a family dinner at the bistro. Just the back room, quiet and casual."

"Esther," Ruth said, "you're a gem."

Her father grunted, but she could tell by the half smile on his lips that he was touched too.

The bistro was closed for the evening, but soon after their arrival, the back room glowed with warm candlelight. In the center of the room, Esther had set a table for eight, already laid with fresh rolls, garlic butter, and pitchers of lemon water. Esther had dismissed her staff for the night, wanting this evening to be intimate, and perhaps the beginning of a Sunday night tradition.

Humming her choir piece, she switched on the last electric votive candle and set it on the table. She was walking toward the kitchen to check on the roast when her phone vibrated in her pocket. It was Rick.

"Please don't cancel," she whispered to herself, then answered. "Hi. Is everything okay?"

"I'm here. Outside." His voice sounded strained. "Just sitting in my truck."

"Is something wrong?" she asked. "Do you want me to come out and help you?"

There was a long pause. "No."

"Then?"

"Do you think it will be okay, Esther? After all this time?"

She thought of their mother's face when she'd mentioned Rick would be coming. And the way their father had pretended not to care but had asked three times if she was sure. The years of silence had cost them all so much.

"Rick, I think it's time. I saw Mom's face. She really wants to see you."

"And Dad?"

"Yes. Him too."

"But what if things don't get better?"

"What if they do?" she asked. "If you don't come in, we'll never know, will we?"

"You're right," he said, "I'll see you in a few."

She clicked off the phone and walked to the door to open it to her brother. He entered, looking freshly showered and a little tired, but wearing a tentative smile.

"An actual shirt?" Esther asked, remarking on the fact that Rick wasn't wearing a T-shirt for once.

"Only the best for family reconciliation," he said, giving her a quick hug. His body was tense but he looked more relaxed than he had sounded moments earlier. "This looks great. I'm almost looking forward to it."

"It will be fine," said Esther, patting him on the back. "Just relax and sit beside me or Cam so we can kick you if things go south."

"Ha," said Rick. "I had no idea I was going to be policed. Maybe I should go." But he was smiling.

"Where is Cam?" she said, looking behind him.

"He's gone to get Brooke. I think they're getting pretty serious. Thanks for inviting her. He wants to introduce her to Dad and Mom."

"Well, he couldn't do much better. She is one of my favorite people."

"I figured if there was company, maybe Dad would behave."

"He's honestly getting much better," said Esther. "I think you'll be pleasantly surprised."

"I hope so," said Rick, turning as the back door opened and Curtis and Anthony came in, followed by Cam and Brooke. They had just finished exchanging greetings and hanging jackets on the nearby coatrack when Ruth came in, smiling wide, rushing to hug first Cam and then Rick.

"Hi, Mom," said Rick, bending down to sweep his mother into his arms.

"Oh, I am so glad to see you," she said, her voice wavering slightly. Her hands trembled as she reached up to touch her son's face, as if confirming he was truly there. "When Cam told me you're staying in town, I was over the moon."

"It's good to see you too, Mom." Esther noticed his eyes were filling with tears. Good tears, she knew. Maybe this evening would go smoothly after all.

Cam noticed his grandfather standing a little apart, watching his wife and son, and walked over to say hello.

"Welcome home, Grandpa," he said. "I wanted to introduce you to my girlfriend, Brooke."

"Hello again," said Brooke.

"It's good to see you," said Ian, smiling at Brooke and Cam. "This young lady used to visit my bistro for thimble cookies, if I remember correctly."

"You remember?" said Brooke. "They were the best thing. Mom would bring me here the Saturday after payday," she told Cam. "It was always a special treat."

"I may even have some on the dessert tray this evening," Esther said as she approached. "Can I take your coat, Dad?"

"Sure," he said, his gaze drifting over to where Rick was still talking to his mother.

"And you remember Curtis? And his son Anthony?" asked Esther.

"Yes," said Ian. "Nice to see you both again."

Esther watched her father's eyes drift again to her brother, and she grasped Curtis's hand. "Come and say hello to Mom," she said. His eyebrows rose, but he followed her.

"Mom, you remember Curtis," she said loudly, pulling her mother's attention away from Rick for a moment.

Her mother turned, looking a little disoriented at the sudden disruption, but she quickly gathered her features and smiled up at Curtis. "I understand that you two are finally dating," said Ruth, and Esther blushed. What was it about parents that made them so embarrassing?

"Yes, she finally decided to give me a chance," said Curtis.

Esther left them to talk and grabbed her brother's arm. "Come on. There's someone you need to say hello to."

Rick looked like he wanted to pull back but allowed himself to be led forward.

"Dad," Rick said.

Ian paused and peered up at Rick. When had their father shrunk so much? Esther wondered. Then she watched her father extend his hand, making the first move, and she could have hugged him. "It's good to see you, son."

Rick hesitated, just for a heartbeat, before grasping the offered hand. "You too, Dad."

It wasn't a big moment. But it was enough for now.

Cam pulled out a chair for Ruth. "Grandma, I hope you're hungry."

"I'm always hungry when Esther's cooking."

As plates began to pass and conversation warmed, even between her brother and her father, Esther sought Curtis's eye. She wanted to share this moment with someone who understood what it meant to rebuild a family from fragments. Someone who knew what this evening meant to her.

Across the table, Curtis seemed to sense her gaze. He looked up from his conversation with her father, and their eyes met. They shared a nod and a smile that felt intimate despite the crowded room, like they both knew this was the beginning of something good. Not just for her family, but for them too.

After dinner, Esther and Rick cleared the table, and she stepped into the other room to get a pot of coffee and the tray of desserts. When she returned, pushing a small cart laden with goodies and side plates, she paused to examine her family. Her mother looked delighted to have her son and her grandson there to speak to. Curtis was still talking to her father, and even Anthony and Brooke seemed to feel relaxed and included.

Maybe I'm getting better at these family gatherings. This one wasn't nearly so tense as the last one.

She walked around, offering coffee and tea and dessert, ending near Curtis and her father.

"Your father has agreed to help us with the bat boxes," he told her.

"Really?" said Cam, picking up on the conversation.

"Really what?" asked Rick.

"I have the funds for the boxes, and I was telling your dad about them," said Curtis. "He's going to come and give us a hand."

"Great," said Rick, looking a little surprised.

"Can I help too?" asked Cam.

"Absolutely," said Rick.

"We can start Wednesday afternoon," said Curtis. "I figure it'll take about… Rick? Three or four hours?"

Rick nodded. "They go together quickly once the boards are cut."

"We can cut them tomorrow or Tuesday," said Curtis. "Then all we need to do is assemble and hammer them together."

"What's a bat box?" asked Brooke.

Cam quietly filled her in, and Anthony said he would join if they needed an extra set of hands.

Esther jumped in. "I'll come along around six with some sandwiches and soup for dinner. You should be nearly done by then."

Curtis lifted his coffee in a toast. "Then we have a plan. Bat boxes and bonding."

They all lifted their cups, but Esther noticed her brother hadn't completely bought in. *Early days*, she thought. *Early days.*

CHAPTER 21

The air in the Men's Shack smelled like sawdust and sunshine as they gathered around the center table on Wednesday afternoon. Each of the five men watched and listened as Curtis showed them all how to assemble the pieces. Rick felt the weight of the hammer in his hand, solid and comforting. It was a tool he understood far better than the complicated emotions creating tension in the room.

"You sure we're doing this right?" Cam asked, when he started to assemble the pup catchers.

"Pretty sure," Rick said. "We made a prototype the other day."

"Okay," said Cam, a little doubtful—until Curtis grabbed said prototype and set it in the middle of the table.

"Here's what it should look like," he said.

"Oh, I see," said Cam, looking at the pieces in front of him and then at the model.

Curtis crossed to where Anthony was working and showed him how to drill the vent holes. Rick caught his father's eye.

"How's it going, Dad?"

"Pretty straightforward," said his father. "When you're finished with the drill, could you pass it to me?" he said to Anthony.

Rick watched his dad handle the tools with practiced ease. It was odd to see this man, whom he thought he knew, working with something other than flour and butter.

"How long have you been working with wood?" he asked, unable to keep the surprise from his voice.

"Since one of my friends told me about The Shack," said Ian. "I joined after my heart attack, and it helped to find others who had gone through similar health issues."

"I didn't know you were a member." He looked at Curtis, and Curtis just shrugged noncommittally. If he didn't know any better, he would think that Curtis and Esther had cooked this whole thing up.

It was the height of meddlesome, but he found he didn't really mind.

When they finished the bat boxes and had begun work on the pup catchers, Esther and Ruth arrived with sandwiches, soup, and a big pot of tea.

"Break time," Ruth said. "These look great."

"I think the community garden will be pleased," said Esther. "I thought you would be able to help Sid out."

Curtis kissed her cheek. "I should have known it was you who suggested us."

"I do my best," said Esther, smiling. She turned to Cam. "Is Brooke coming?"

"No, she's at work tonight," he said. "Not sure bats are her thing."

"Maybe she'll come for the opening ceremony after they're mounted," said Esther.

"Maybe," said Cam. "Depends on when it is, I guess."

"Cam may not be here either," said Anthony. "We have to be on location up-island by Monday."

"You're leaving so soon?" said Ruth, looking a little sad.

"No worries, Gram. I'll be back in a few weeks, in time for Sunday dinner."

"Well, when you come, it will be at our house," said Ruth.

Rick glanced at Esther to see how she felt about being usurped, but she was smiling happily.

"Come on, you lot, let's clear up here and eat," Esther said, and soon they were sharing a meal together for the second time that week.

When they were done, they finished assembling the last of the pup catchers, and Ian stood beside Rick, admiring their work.

"This was good," said Ian.

Rick nodded, looking over at his father. "Yeah, it really was."

"They all turned out solid," said his father. "Nice work."

Rick waited, expecting his father to add a "but" to the end of the sentence, but it never came.

"Everyone did a good job," said his father. "We should do something like this again."

"You don't happen to know anything about wood turning, do you?" asked Rick.

"I'm not great at it, but I'm willing to learn. There are a few members who teach it if you have the patience."

"Well, that's what I'm learning now," said Rick.

"I've had more experience with the metal lathe," said his father. "But they are similar."

"Didn't know you were good with your hands, Dad."

"I was a baker and a jack-of-all-trades in the bistro."

"Yes, I suppose you were at that. In fact, it's probably where I first became interested in the trades."

"It's been a good career for you, Rick. I'm sorry I tried to foist my dreams on you. I've always regretted that. And being so hard on Esther too."

Rick felt a lump growing in his throat and fought to swallow it down.

"Thanks for saying that, Dad. I appreciate it."

They were still admiring the bat boxes, but the tension Rick had felt in recent years when he thought about his father had vanished.

"I had a lot of time to think when I was waiting for my heart surgery." His father's voice softened, so Rick was forced to lean in to hear what he was saying. Ian traced the edge of the bat box with his finger, not meeting Rick's eyes. "When you're facing a surgery like that, you think of things you regret." He paused, and Rick waited for him to continue. Needing to hear what he would say next. "I thought about how much I regretted missing so much of your life. Your life, and Sean's and Cam's lives."

"I've missed you too, Dad," he said.

His father turned toward him. "And I want to thank you for looking out for your sister back…" His voice cracked, and he swept his hand in the air instead of completing the sentence.

"When she was with Seth?" Rick asked, finishing his father's thought.

Ian nodded, his eyes cast down again. "I had no idea he would treat her that way."

"None of us did," said Rick, reaching toward his father but then withdrawing his hand again, letting it fall against his thigh.

"I shouldn't have cut her off like that. I should have supported her. But I was so angry…"

"It was a long time ago, Dad, and she seems happy with Curtis. I think he'll treat her well."

"Yes, I think so too," said his father. "And she has done well with the business."

Rick nodded in agreement.

Ian looked at him again. "I'm sorry your marriage ended, son."

"It's okay," said Rick. "Sometimes things aren't meant to last that long."

"Yes, I suppose so," said his father. "I'm grateful I still have your mother. Not sure what I'd do without her."

"Mom is one of a kind, Dad," said Rick. "You are lucky."

"Yes," said his father, looking out at the yard behind the Shack. "Well, it's been a long day, and I'm still getting over jet lag. I'll see you soon?"

"Sunday night, by the sounds of it, if not sooner."

"Until Sunday, then."

He watched his father walk over to collect his mother and suggest it was time to leave.

Esther joined him. "Everything okay, big brother?"

"Early days, Esther. But, yeah, things are moving in the right direction."

"Oh, good." She reached up and hugged him, and he gave her a quick hug back.

"Still not a huggy family, sis."

"We'll work on it," she laughed.

EPILOGUE

Curtis and Rick were on the couch, half watching a show and waiting for Esther to get ready for the choir performance, when Pearl, with her usual feline stealth, leaped up and proceeded to plant herself firmly between them. Without missing a beat, she laid her front paw possessively on Rick's knee.

Rick raised an eyebrow, looking equal parts amused and trapped. "Uh… she's touching me."

Curtis grinned, reaching over to scratch behind Pearl's ear. "I'd take it as a compliment. She usually swats first."

Rick gave a dry chuckle and held up a crinkly package. "I might have had a bit of help."

Curtis leaned in for a better look. "Salmon treats?"

Rick shrugged. "Sometimes people—and cats—just need a little nudge."

At that moment, the hallway door creaked open, and Esther appeared, brushing away a strand of hair that refused to cooperate.

"You look nice," said Curtis.

"Thanks," she said. Then she stopped, one hand firmly on her hip. "What's going on here?"

"We're making friends," said Curtis.

"I'm so glad she's accepted you both after all."

"Kind of," Rick said, holding up the treat bag like it was a peace offering.

Esther rolled her eyes, but there was affection behind it. "I should have known there was something more. You let yourself be bribed, did you?" She walked over and patted Pearl.

Curtis rose carefully, nudging Pearl off his lap. She let

out a small meow of protest but didn't flee. Progress. He offered Esther his hand.

"You ready?" he asked.

She looked at him—then at Rick, who was already pulling on his jacket—and smiled. "Almost. Rick, I told Yvonne we could give her a ride. Do you mind seeing if she's ready?"

"Sure," he said with a grin.

"What are you up to?" asked Curtis, after Rick had left.

"What are you talking about?" she said, eyes wide. "Just giving my neighbor a ride."

"You are matchmaking again, aren't you?"

She chuckled. "Some people need a nudge in the right direction." She looked at her watch. "I think we can go now."

Curtis shook his head and followed Esther out the door to find Yvonne and Rick in conversation. Yvonne, Curtis noticed, was glowing under Rick's attention.

As they walked toward the car, Esther's hand brushed Curtis's and instead of pulling away, she let it linger.

Curtis looked over at Esther and smiled. It was hard to believe how much could change in just a few short weeks.

Even if some of those changes were still unfolding, he felt certain they were heading in the right direction. Small signs like Pearl's paw on a knee, and like Esther shared confidences, meant the walls were softening.

They were building something.

Something grounded in trust.

A new beginning.

Together.

Author's Note

Dear Reader,

I hope you enjoyed *Whisking Love and Building Dreams*! If you'd like to spend more time in the charming island town of Sunshine Bay—with its quirky characters, lovable cats, and heartfelt stories—be sure to explore the *Sunshine Bay* series.

Want to meet more of the downtown business owners? Check out the *Shops at Sunshine Bay* books for more cozy small-town charm.

To stay in the loop about upcoming releases, special offers, and behind-the-scenes peeks, visit www.jeaninelauren.com and sign up for my newsletter.

Until next time,

Happy Reading!

Jeanine

P.S.

If you enjoyed Esther and Curtis's story, I'd be so grateful if you'd take a moment to leave a review. Reader reviews are a wonderful way to support indie authors like me—and they help others discover stories they might love, too. Thank you!

ABOUT THE AUTHOR

Jeanine Lauren is a *USA Today* bestselling author who writes heartwarming women's fiction and sweet romance filled with friendship, love, community, and second chances.

After a lifetime of writing for school, work, and those never-ending to-do lists, Jeanine followed her passion and published *Love's Fresh Start* in 2019—the first book in her *Sunshine Bay* series. Since then, she's been making up for lost time, writing as fast as she can to bring more of Sunshine Bay to life.

Want to know when the next book is coming out? Join her newsletter for updates, sneak peeks, and more at www.jeaninelauren.com.

Jeanine lives in the lower mainland of British Columbia, just a stone's throw from the fictional seaside town of Sunshine Bay, where her characters' stories unfold.

9 781997 523093